To my wife "Corrine"
without her
"nothing."

Assumptions Can Kill

PAGE PUBLISHING, INC.
New York, NY

First originally published by Page Publishing, Inc. 2018

ISBN 978-1-64138-706-4 (Paperback)
ISBN 978-1-64138-707-1 (Digital)

Printed in the United States of America

Chapter 1

I wonder just what the hell this is all about, Jake thought to himself for a third time in the last five minutes, and the twentieth time since he'd gotten the call. The alarm bells were going off in his head, that's for sure—but why? The *why* was eluding him! Was it the tone of Cammila's voice when he'd answered his phone, or just the fact she'd even called him at home?

Again, he went over the call from Cammila in his head. Cammila Martinez was a computer analysist at Wineca High School where Jake was a part-time custodian on the 6:00 to 10:00 p.m. shift.

Jake had answered the phone, "Hello, who's this?" He heard, "Hey, Jake, it's me, Cammie." This grabbed his attention instantly because he always called her Cammila no matter how many times she had told him to call her Cammie; and as such, she insisted on calling him Mr. O'Nell no matter how many times he had told her to call him Jake, that Mr. O'Nell was his dad.

Jake paused a couple of seconds then answered, "Hey, what's up, Cammie?" He knew he'd answered correctly when she said, with obvious relief in her voice, "I need a huge favor," asking him if he could come in right now and help her move the desks and tables in the learning lab. "I know you'll be coming in at six, but with the kids gone on Christmas break, I wanted to get things arranged for the new laptops. "Well," answered Jake, "I suppose I can, but what about Bob, isn't he there?" Bob Haley was Jake's boss, and he worked 10:00 a.m. to 6:30 p.m. each day.

Cammie had hesitated a little before answering, "Bob didn't come in today. He called in sick." Then she added, "But look, if it is too much trouble, I suppose I could get Carl to help." She went on quickly before Jake could answer, with "If you come in, I'll treat you to some of those hotdogs we both love so much! So, Jake, how about it?" That's when Jake knew something was really wrong!

First of all, his boss, Bob, had never called in sick one day in his life. Everybody said he was too damn mean to let any germ get to him. Second, Jake had just talked to him two hours ago to make their weekly bet on the games coming up over the weekend. Then her last part about the hotdogs, Cammila hated them! The two of them had gotten into the habit of taking lunch break together the past two years, and one thing Cammila had made clear was how much she disliked hotdogs, which just happened to be one of Jake's favorite foods. "Lips and assholes," she would say, and Jake would answer, "You bet, nothing but the best parts!"

Jake took a second then answered, "Okay, I'll come to your rescue just like a knight in shining armor," laughing as he said it. Cammie answered with a nervous laugh. "Don't make it sound so serious. Just come in the back door." Then she added, "Well, if we had a back door. Bye-bye." Jake barely had time to say "okay" before the line went dead.

Chapter 2

Driving to the school, Jake was sure of two things; first, someone was listening to Cammila's every word, and second, the last bit about the back door was a warning. Wineca High had a front door and actually two back doors, but they were mainly used to bring in supplies, or visiting teams came in that way to reach the locker rooms.

Jake had survived twelve years of being a marine sniper, and his instinct had saved his life more than once, so he was not about to ignore the warning bells going off in his head now. He reached down and touched the handle of his combat knife, again wondering if he should have grabbed his pistol. Once again thinking, *Nah, if things were really bad, Cammila would have said even more.*

It was a decision he would later regret for a long, long time.

Jake's drive to the school normally took twenty minutes if he took the main highway. The school itself was a half mile off the main highway on its own driveway and was a good thirty-minute drive from the town of Wineca. The school was built on land donated, along with the money to build the school, by a rich bachelor who wanted to leave something nice for his friends and neighbors. No one complained of the drive; the location was beautiful, overlooking the town way below.

Once you turned onto the school driveway, it led directly to a huge parking lot that went around the front and east side of the school. On the south side was a smaller lot where supply trucks and buses parked for the back doors. There were some emergency exit doors as well. But Jake had another option. It was ten minutes longer to take the gravel town road that led to a small parking lot and picnic area located two hundred feet from the school, but it was shielded from the school by a dozen rows of huge pine trees, and only a few people even knew it was there. Bob and Jake used it on occasion when they wanted to sneak into the school and work on projects without being bothered.

There was also another reason Jake decided to use the secluded parking lot. It led to a secret entrance that he and Bob had decided to keep to themselves. From the outside, it opened into a small storage room for lawn care items, but it had a hidden door into the school that led into a supply room. Only three people knew it was there, Bob, himself, and his Uncle Caleb.

As Jake parked his truck, he thought to himself, *It's been a long time since I've been wired up like this,* and he felt good—but then the doubt crept in. Was he reading too much into Cammila's words? Thinking on it more, he decided there were two possibilities. The first, that Rink was up to no good again. Carl Rink was the school's Principal. Carl was forty-five years old and never married. He hated Jake from day 1, mostly because Jake took no shit from him. Rink had given Cammila trouble once before, and if he was giving her trouble again, this time, Jake was not going to stand by and do nothing, regardless of any consequences. The other possibility, Jake thought, *Maybe she's done waiting for you to make a move.* She'd been flirting with him more and more the last six months. Jake wasn't stupid, but he was fifteen years older than her, and he hadn't even thought of anyone but Korrine for so long; he wasn't exactly sure how to go about things. Cammila was drop-dead gorgeous, so the thought of her being interested in him caught him off guard.

Jake laughed as he looked at himself in the rearview mirror thinking, *Oh, you bet, old man, that's it for sure. She's just waiting for you to make love to her in the computer lab.* Jake was still laughing to himself as he put his truck keys above the passenger-side sun visor and, as usual, left it unlocked. He figured if somebody wanted to steal his old rust bucket of a truck, they could have it.

Jake carefully walked through the pines and slipped quietly into the school. He slowly opened the door from the supply room to the main hall, looking left and right. Seeing nothing, he went across the main hall to the central maintenance room, which also had offices for him and Bob.

Jake was again on edge. A school was a quiet, lonely place when most or all the people had left. A fact Jake enjoyed, but once in a while, you could sense when things were out of place, and this was one of those times.

Chapter 3

Jake had decided to check the maintenance office first to see if Bob had left him a note, which he did once in a while if he had to leave early. Jake opened the door and slipped in, flipping on the main light switch. Jake spotted Bob by his desk with his reading lamp on. Jake started to say, "Hey, boss, what's going on?" But he never finished because Bob was sitting in his chair, his head back so far that Jake knew he was dead. As Jake neared Bob, he could see Bob's throat had been cut deep and from ear to ear. As Jake looked at the brutal jagged cut, he was sure of one thing. That the cut was made with a combat knife similar to his own, but bigger, much bigger. Jake had seen this kind of kill too many times, some by his own hands. Now the marine sniper in Jake came to full alert. Deciding on his next move, he knew he could sneak back out and get help. That is, if he could convince Conner Hess, the sheriff, to believe him. Their history together was bad, and even if Conner believed him, the more important issue was Cammila. Jake knew the man who did this to Bob wouldn't hesitate to do the same to her. Jake had no idea what this was all about, but he would bet Cammila was in deep shit, and that was why she had tried to warn him. Someone wanted him to come in and walk right into a trap. He knew that there would be a person or persons waiting for him at each of the doors; it was the only thing that fit.

Jake looked at the back wall thinking of what was behind it, then, shaking his head, he decided to find Cammila first. Jake left the room deciding to check the side door first; it was the closest, and the one he mostly used. Still being cautious, Jake didn't go down the main hall. He used a roundabout way into the science room. It had a door from which he could see all the way to the door of the outside entrance. Opening the door a crack, Jake couldn't believe what he was seeing. There was a big man dressed in Army gear waiting just inside the door, hiding behind the Christmas tree there. He was holding a large combat knife similar to Jake's, but larger, much larger. There was a second man sitting behind Cammila, who was standing at the entrance counter where visitors had to stop and register. The man was holding a gun pointed at Cammila's back. Jake figured the plan was that they expected him to come in through the door as usual, head toward Cammila, not thinking anything was wrong, and the big man would jump him, cutting his throat like old Bob's.

Jake's first thought was *Son of a bitch*, had Cammila not warned him, they could both be dead right now, and that really pissed him off. As he carefully eased the door shut, Jake thought, *I'm going to give you bastards one hell of a surprise. Or at least try to.*

He went down across the science lab to the door that opened into a small office next to the registration corner, praying it was unlocked. He knew how loud a key can sometimes be.

Jake's good luck was holding as the doorknob turned easily in his hand. He opened it a crack, thinking, *All I have to do is get to the guy by Cammila, kill him, take his gun, shoot the guy with the knife, then run like hell with Cammila. Piece of cake! Yeah right, old man.* He looked down at his hands thinking they might be shaking, but no, steady as a rock. Jake realized just how alive he was feeling, like warriors have always felt. Scared to the core with hearts racing, ready to face whatever came their way. Jake had been moving even as he thought all that, and now he was by the doorway to the counter, only eight feet from his target, thinking of nothing more now than how his next move had to be done without noise or hesitation. He paused, wondering for a brief second if he could do it—not that he had a problem with killing, he'd done his share in Iraq and Afghanistan, and he'd been good, very good. Not that he enjoyed killing, far from it, but he knew that it was something that had to be done. Like now, but he wondered, was he still good enough? Then he thought, *Piss on it. You've got to do it. Now get it done, old man!*

Jake sneaked one last peek to make sure his target was still in the same place. It was a slight risk, but he'd been taught to be sure of your position before making your move. He also wanted to make sure the man was holding the gun in his right hand. If the SOB was left-handed, he might have to take a bullet before getting to the man. Jake made his move; the gun was still in his target's right hand. As he moved, it was as if time had slipped into slow motion. Jake was moving quietly and as fast as he could, but whether it was a noise that Jake had made or instinct, his target whirled around, and Jake heard a "phet" sound and felt a sting on his earlobe. Then Jake was on him, pushing the gun aside with his left hand and plunging the knife with his right hand into his opponent's throat, all the way to the hilt. Jake pulled the gun from the dying man's hand and turned toward the big man by the door, and none too soon, because for the size of the guy, he was fast, almost unbelievably fast. He was already jumping over the counter when Jake shot him in the face three times as fast as he could pull the trigger. Even then, mortally wounded, he almost stuck the knife into Jake's chest, the blade sliding along his side as the big man landed almost on top of his partner. The whole thing had taken fifteen to twenty seconds tops, and with the gun having a silencer, there had been almost no noise.

The quiet was shattered by Cammila's scream. That woke Jake up out of his stupor. He'd been just standing there amazed he was still alive, thankful he'd pulled it off with just a couple of scratches.

Jake grabbed Cammila's arm and pulled her toward the outside doors. "It's okay, Cammila, it's me, Jake." But she wouldn't move and was getting ready to scream again. That's when Jake slapped her hard, yelling at her, "Knock it off. We've no time for this shit!"

She stood there, stunned, then slapped Jake back. Much to his surprise, she said, "Goddam it, Jake, for the last time, call me *Cammie!* Not Cammila."

Then in a more normal tone, she asked, "Jesus, Jake, what the hell is going on, and how the hell did you do that?" Jake started to answer when he spotted a young Latino man coming through the entrance doors carrying a shotgun, the very doors that Jake had planned on using for their escape. Jake pulled Cammie down behind the counter and whispered to her, "Listen, Cammie, when I say go, run to the band room. The door's unlocked. Don't look back, just run, okay?" Cammie nodded.

Just inside the doors, the young man yelled, "Spiker, Ricky, where the hell are you? Sarge says to be ready, that O'Nell should be here any minute. Hey, you bastards better not be screwing with that gal. I told you I get her first!"

Jake yelled, "Run, Cammie, run!" as he jumped up, firing two quick shots at the young man, hitting the Christmas tree and making bulbs explode. The man yelled, "What the hell!" as he dove to the floor with the shotgun falling to the side, exactly as Jake had hoped would happen.

Jake took off running for the band room, catching up to Cammie just as she opened the door. It had only been a forty-foot run, but it had seemed like a mile. Jake ducked in behind Cammie, pulling the door shut and locking it just as the shotgun pellets hammered the door. The shotgun sounded like a damn cannon compared to the silenced .22 Jake was using. As soon as they'd ducked into the room, Jake yelled, "Cammie, stop!" She did. Jake pushed her down next to him behind a large garbage can just inside the door and put his hand over her mouth. He whispered into her ear, "Listen, if you want to live through the next five minutes, no matter what, you can't make a sound, okay?" Cammie, with her eyes wide, nodded her okay. Jake pushed her down even farther and said again, "No noise or we're dead!"

Just then, they heard the young man try the door, saying "Shit!" He blew the lock out then kicked the door open, switching to Spanish as he did so and making the mistake Jake had hoped for—pumping in his next round as he came into the room, not taking the time to do it before entering.

As the young man came in, he desperately tried to finish chambering a round and shoot Jake, but he stood no chance. Jake had stood up and opened fired into the young man's face. The first round caught him in the cheek, the next two directly into his forehead. The young man slumped back against the door frame, dropping the shotgun to the floor. Jake would have shot him again, but the gun had clicked empty.

Jake threw down the pistol and scooped up the shotgun. Turning around, he grabbed Cammie just as she was either going to scream or throw up. Jake gave her no chance to do either as he pulled her with him, yelling, "We have to move, Cammie, in case there's more of them! Come on, I know a safe place."

They left the band room again without seeing anyone. Cammie still had the look of shock on her face as he pushed her into the huge maintenance room. Jake didn't lock the door, knowing that would be a dead giveaway if someone came looking for them.

Cammie was just ahead of Jake, spotting Bob by his desk. Cammie ran toward him, yelling, "Bob, are you okay? I didn't know where they'd taken you. Bob—" She reached out to touch his shoulder. Jake tried to stop her, but he was a second too late. As she grabbed Bob's shoulder, his body slid to the floor, and his head rolled back, exposing the jagged cut.

Jake clamped his hand over her mouth just as she started to scream. Cammie fought Jake hard, but he held on like a giant vise. "Listen, Cammie, I know this is tough to take, but if you scream and there are more of them, we'll die too. It's that simple." Jake went on in a quiet soothing voice, "Come on, Cammie, help me out here. Now are there any more of those men? Please, Cammie."

After a few more seconds, Cammie quit struggling and pried Jake's hand off her mouth. She said, "You're right, Jake, I won't scream anymore. And yes, there are more men up front and by the other doors. I'm sorry for screaming before. It's—"

Jake stopped her and said, "You've nothing to be sorry for, kid. It's been a bitch of a day so far. First things first, I have a place to hide, and we can talk there and decide on our options, okay?" Cammie nodded, and Jake led her to the back wall.

Chapter 4

At that moment, the men Cammie had told Jake about were standing around the bodies he had left behind. The leader of the group was a big black American, dressed similarly to the two bodies behind the desk Jake had killed first. The men called him Sarge. He turned to face the school's principal, Carl Rink. Sarge had disliked the weasel-nosed bastard the minute they'd met. Sarge knew the type, a real asshole who thought they were smarter than everyone else, talking big, but a coward inside.

Rink wasn't looking so smug as he had two to three hours ago when they first met. Sarge glared at Rink, saying, "Listen, you piece of shit, you told us this guy was an old drunk and that there were only six ways into this school, and we covered them. Now this guy comes in unseen, takes out two of my best men, and then kills Raul's nephew like it was nothing. A piece of cake, you said. Raul is on his way, and this whole deal is screwed from the start. What you got to say now, smart-ass?"

Rink finally found his voice, answering him in a whine, "I don't understand. How could O'Nell do this? He must have some help, that has to be it." Rink asked Sarge, "Jesus, what are you going to do now?"

Sarge yelled at him, "I'll tell you, fuckhead. First, you're going to call your brother. Tell him to get his ass up here *now!* After you make the call, pull the plug on the phones so O'Nell can't call for any more help. Cells don't work here, right?"

Rink nodded and said, "They won't work inside at all, and only a couple spots outside gets reception."

Sarge said, "Okay, now move your ass, Rink. Go around front and do what I said. Oh, and one more thing. You better start praying that Raul kills you quick—not slow, real slow."

"Jesus," Rink said again, taking off at a run on the outside sidewalk heading to the front offices.

Sarge called out to the last of his own men he'd brought, "Steve, you go around the outside of this school. Find out where or how this SOB got in. When you do, I want you to rig it in case he tries to get out the same way or if anybody else tries to get in."

"Okay," Steve said. "Will do! Anything else?"

"Yeah!" Sarge said as he turned to Paco, one of the four men who'd come with Emille, Raul Vortez's nephew, who's now dead. "What was the name of this guy?"

Paco answered, "Rink called him Jake O'Nell."

Sarge asked Steve, "You ever hear that name in the service?"

Steve answered, "Maybe, but nobody special comes to mind."

"Okay," Sarge said. "I'm going around front. Paco, you're with me. The rest of you outside. Watch the doors. Anyone comes out, you shoot to kill."

Steve had paused outside the doors before going around the school, thinking to himself, *Maybe I should have told Sarge, yeah, I've heard of a Jake O'Nell.* But until he was sure, he was going to keep quiet. If this was *that* Jake O'Nell, this was going to be no piece of cake. Steve said to himself, "What, oh what has Mrs. Garvey's boy gotten himself into this time? What a mess!"

Sarge was thinking the same thought as he went around front with Paco, *What a mess, a big fucking mess!*

Chapter 5

Jake was having the same thoughts that Sarge had just voiced as he led Cammie to the back wall. Cammie asked, "We're not going to just hide in here, are we? They'll find us for sure."

Jake said, "Just watch" as he reached under the bottom shelf and then pulled the shelf and wall toward him, much to Cammie's surprise. Jake said, "Come on" and led her into a good-sized room. Jake pulled the hidden door shut behind him and turned on more lights. Cammie looked around. One whole wall was covered with TV monitor screens; on the other side was a bed, a kitchenette, and a small door in the back that Jake said was a bathroom.

Taking it all in, Cammie asked, "What is this place?"

Jake said, "Listen, Cammie, I'll tell you all about it, but first, you tell me how this whole thing started, and just how many more bad guys did you see?"

"Well," she said, "there was like eight or ten all together, and Jake, Carl's involved too. I came in like normal and about an hour later, Rink calls me to his office. They'd caught Bob already. When I got there, that Ricky guy grabbed me, and Carl told me to call you in. Bob told me not to, but they said they would kill Bob if I didn't. So I called. I'm sorry. I tried to warn you with our names and hotdog thing. I didn't know what else to do!"

Jake said, "Hey, it's all right, Cammie, you did great. You saved both our lives. Now let's call for some help." He picked up the phone and thought about dialing 911, but he would just get Mae, Wineca's dispatcher, and she would call the sheriff before sending help. So Jake dialed Connor Hess's cell phone. He was the sheriff of Crawfish

County. Hess answered on the second ring with "Sheriff Hess, how can I help you?"

"Hey, Connor. It's me, Jake."

There was a pause and then Connor yelled, "Jake, what the hell do you want? And how the hell did you get this number?"

Jake answered, "It doesn't matter how I got the number. Just shut the hell up and listen. Are you at Caleb's?"

"I am," Connor said, "and don't tell me to shut up, you asshole, and how did you know where I'm at?"

Jake said, "It's Friday. You have supper and play cards with Caleb every Friday evening since Hazel died. Okay, now listen. First, tell Caleb 'Alamo.' Second, I'm at the school with Cammila Martinez, and something big and bad is going down here. Bob is *dead*. I had to kill three bad asses who were holding Cammila, but there's a lot more of them, and Carl Rink's in on it with them—"

Connor cut in with a cold voice, saying, "It sounds like you've been drinking again. I hope, Jake, you haven't done anything stupid, or I'll really bust your ass this time. So how about just sleeping it off, and we'll forget all about this call, okay?"

Jake yelled back, "CONNOR, you dumb bastard. I'm not drunk. Here, I'll let you talk to Ms. Martinez." Jake handed the phone to Cammie, saying, "Talk to this ape, will you?"

She grabbed the phone and said, "Sheriff, you've got to listen!" She said it again and then looked at Jake, saying, "It's dead. There's no dial tone."

"What?" Jake said, taking the phone, listening and trying to call. "Shit, they must have cut the lines," he said, giving the phone a toss against the wall.

Cammie asked, "Do you think he'll come for us?"

Jake looked her in the eye and said, "I don't know, Cammie. Connor and I have a history, and it's not good, but he's a damn good sheriff, so maybe, just maybe, he'll come. For now, we'll be safe here. Only three people know of this place besides me, so let's turn on these cameras and see what Rink is up to."

Carl Rink, Jake thought to himself, *what an asshole.* Jake had never thought much of the man from day 1, so it was no real surprise he was involved in whatever was going on here.

Jake turned to Cammie. "Tell me again, how many men did you see, and did they say anything about what's going on?"

Cammie answered, "Not really. The only thing other than getting you was, I heard the leader of the men that were dressed as soldiers say to that young Latino, Emille, that the trucks are here. He answered, 'Good, as soon as we take care of this O'Nell problem, we'll get down to business.' God, it was awful, Jake. Emille's the one who said they just had some business to do, and we could all go free after it was done. Bob told me, 'Don't listen to them, Cammila, they're lying.' The guy with the knife, they called him Spiker, he said, 'Shut up, old man.' And then Rink just hauls off and punches Bob, laughing, and told Bob, 'You don't know how long I've waited to do that you, you ornery old bastard!' Bob spits out some blood and says to Rink, 'You're a big man when I'm all tied up, but you tell these SOBs to let me loose. I'll show you how this old man can kick your ass.' He even asked the one they called Sarge, 'How about it, big man. Just let me loose for two minutes, just two minutes.' They all started to laugh, and Emille yelled, 'Enough' and then made me call you.

"Again, Jake, I'm sorry. Can you forgive me?"

Jake said, "For the last time, Cammie, you did great. You managed to warn me without them knowing a thing."

As Cammie started to cry, Jake went to her, giving her a hug, saying, "Enough, you did great, okay."

They stood there locked in a hug, not saying anything, both deep in thought for a minute or so. Then Cammie pushed away and said, "I still don't know how you did that so fast, killing those first two and then shooting that young man, Emille, right in the face. He didn't have a chance, did he—I mean, couldn't we have just run away?"

Jake looked at her and said in a cold, rough voice she'd never heard before, "You're joking, right? First, how I did it is because I'm an ex-marine, twelve years in the Corp., a sniper, and today I was lucky. Those first two were very good. They didn't expect me to fight, or I would be dead now, and maybe you too, or worse. Did you forget about the 'taking turns screwing' you and he 'got you first' part from that young man, as you called him? He was no kid. You don't get to be boss of guys like these by being nice. He knew how to use this shotgun, didn't he, and yeah, I shot him in the face and head. They taught me in the Marines to take out an enemy as quickly and permanently as possible. Just suppose I'd shot him in the chest, and he had a vest on. We would be dead right now. I know fighting dirty isn't politically correct nowadays, but those who hesitate, *die*. Not to mention the fact that maybe you can outrun a shotgun shell, but I know damn well I can't. Lastly, in that room behind us is a very old friend of mine, murdered in cold blood. Yeah, he was one ornery bastard, but he was family to me. Maybe you should think on that a second and be damn glad you're alive!"

Jake said no more, sitting down in a swivel chair, turning toward the TV monitors and turning on switches. Cammie was quiet a moment then said, "I'm so sorry, Jake, you're right. I am glad, very glad I'm alive, so please forgive my stupidity. This is like having a nightmare you can't wake up from. Okay, from now on, I'll do what you say, help if I can, and no more screaming."

"Fair enough," he said without turning around. Then he continued, "Now let's see who our friends are and what this is all about."

Cammie asked Jake, "What the heck is all this? I thought there was only a camera by each door with the monitor in the main office."

Jake said, "That's what the owner of the school wanted everyone to think. That way, we can keep an eye on things so there will never be a Sandy Hook here. We don't have them in the locker rooms or bathrooms, nothing perverted like that, but the rest of the school and parking lots are covered. Like I said, the owner of this school wanted it kept safe, so this room was built in secret. Bob and I and two others help keep an eye on things." Jake asked Cammie, "Are we okay on this?"

Cammie answered, "Yes, I think I understand."

"Good. Now let's see what Rink's up to." He pointed to the screen that said "Office."

Cammie looked at the screen and pointed. "That man with him, that's the one they call Sarge."

Jake replied, "Let's see what they're saying. We can hear them, but they can't hear us unless I want them to. Boy, it sure doesn't look like they like each other, does it?"

Rink's voice came through the speaker yelling, "He's on his way, for Christ's sake, and you are not going to pin this on me. Emille said you and your men were good and would handle the security!"

Sarge yelled back, "This was supposed to be a normal safe operation, only an old man to deal with, and then we get here and that woman shows up. Then you and Emille tell me we have to call this part-time custodian in ASAP without saying why! So I go along because Emille asked me to. He said it was important, and you assured us that all we had to deal with was a drunken old bum. But a drunk doesn't take out my two best men, free the girl, and kill Emille in less than five minutes. So I'll tell you what, Mr. Big-Shot Principal, when Raul gets here, I'm telling him right up front how I screwed up and ask him to forgive me for letting his nephew get killed. But you, Mr. Rink, and your goddamn brother better have one damn good reason for screwing this whole operation up and be man enough to tell him."

Then they heard a loud, deep voice saying, "Bravo, Sergeant, bravo! That was well said." The voice was coming from a fiftyish Latino gentleman as he came through the door from the hall. He was flanked by two able-looking Latino bodyguards. Again, he said, "Bravo, Sergeant Michael, that was well said, and you have nothing to fear from me. My man, Paco, had enough sense to call me and tell me what went on here today. You did your job as well as Emille and Mr. Rink would let you. It seems this asshole, Rink, and his brother talked my nephew into something that I was not told about, and it got my Emille killed."

Facing Rink, the man called Raul said, "Now, Mr. Rink, are you going to tell me what this was about and what went wrong, or should I have Paco shoot you in your guts so you die in much pain and slowly. Then when your brother gets here, we'll get our answers from him."

Jake and Cammie could see how shaken Rink was; he was terrified of this man, Raul. But finally, he found his voice, starting out slowly and carefully, knowing his life was on the line with each word. Rink said, "It is an honor to finally meet you, Mr. Vortez. It's true my brother and I talked Emille into having this Jake O'Nell come in and have him killed before you got here. It was to be a surprise, a bonus from Emille, myself, and my brother. A gift to get our operation together off to a good start, if you will, because if O'Nell's dead, it would be worth a lot of money for us."

"Indeed?" asked Raul. "How much money?"

Rink answered, "I don't know for sure. My brother and Emille didn't share those details with me. My brother will be here any minute to clear this whole mess up."

Raul replied, "You, Mr. Rink, have five minutes. If your brother is not here by then, Paco here will shoot you in your fat stomach with his little .22. It will be quite painful. Now, Sergeant Michael, your suggestions on how to proceed from here?"

Rink just sat listening as Sarge told Raul, "First, we hunt the woman and O'Nell down and kill them, then proceed as planned."

"Agreed," said Raul. Rink smiled at the thought of Cammie and O'Nell finally dead.

Chapter 6

Jake and Cammie had listened to the exchange. Jake was thinking, *Mr. Rink, you are so dead, first chance I get!*

Jake broke the silence saying, "I never did like that asshole, Rink." Swiveling his chair to face Cammie, he added, "I didn't even know he had a brother, and to be mixed up with Raul Vortez. He's the biggest drug dealer in North America. If he's here, this is all about drugs for sure."

"Do you know him?" asked Cammie.

Jake answered, "Not hardly, but I'm kind of a news junkie."

Cammie said, "Okay, that's well and good. We know who that is and, now, what this is about—well, sort of, but didn't you just hear them? They're going to hunt us down and kill us! Don't you think we should try and get out now?"

"Listen," said Jake, "we're safe here. We have food and water, a bathroom, and in the cabinet there above the bed is enough weapons and ammo to hold them off if I had to. Plus, we can see where they're at and what they're doing. Cammie, you don't have to worry. With Bob dead, there's only two others now who know of this place. My godfather, Caleb Johnson—he's with the sheriff right now playing cribbage unless I did get through to that knucklehead sheriff, and they're on their way here. The last one who knows about this place is Pastor Dean from Heaven's Church, and he called me this morning to tell me he was going out of town for a few days, so we'll just—"

Cammie interrupted, "But, Jake—" She was staring at the screens.

Jake said, "No buts now, Cammie, we're going to stay here and that's that!"

"No!" yelled Cammie. "Turn around, Jake! Isn't that Pastor Dean?"

Jake spun around saying, "What the hell is he doing here?"

Jake had turned the sound off when he was talking with Cammie. He reached over and turned it back on, still not believing what he was seeing on the screen. Pastor Dean was walking over to Raul, saying, "It is good to see you again, Mr. Vortez. I have to apologize for being late. I was administering the last rites to one of my flock, as it were, and he was in no hurry to meet his maker."

Sarge yelled, "Preacher, I don't give a shit why you're late. You have some explaining to do to Mr. Vortez, and I have to go find this O'Nell in one hell of a big school. It's going to take time, which we might not have a lot of."

As he turned to go, Dean said, "Hey, soldier boy, cool your jets. O'Nell's going to be no problem. He's not going anywhere."

Sarge turned on Dean, saying, "You ever call me that again, and you're dead. Do you understand, preacher man? You call me Mr. Michael or Sergeant Michael."

"Enough!" yelled Raul. "Pastor Dean, my trucks are here, and you arrived in time to save your brother, but now it's time to talk."

At that moment, Sarge's man, Steve, came through the front doors and yelled, "Sarge, I found it! There's a small access door behind the AC units with a hidden door into a storage room that goes into the main hall, and I did like you said."

Pastor Dean surprised everyone by turning around and facing up to a small ceiling light and saying, "Well, Jake old boy, a secret you kept from me. That wasn't very nice, but as you can see, I kept some from you as well. I'd like you to meet my brother, Carl Rink. You see, Chadfee is our mother's maiden name, and I'd like you to meet our business partner, Mr. Raul Vortez. You see, people?" Dean said, turning back to the others, "Jake O'Nell has this hidden security room with cameras to watch and hear your every word.

"Oh, and Jake," Dean continued, turning back to face the camera, "don't bother looking for the guns. I stopped by this morning and took them, along with the master security gate key, so you can't

24

trap us either. So you are truly screwed, Jake. I don't know why you didn't just come in and die like we had planned for you to do."

Raul said, "Dean, what the hell is going on here? I want answers now. Are you crazy, talking to the ceiling?"

"No, Mr. Vortez, I'm not crazy. You see, Jake O'Nell, he owns this school and about everything else in this hicksville corner of the state. He's the sole owner of SSBBKO Enterprises, and he was nice enough to bequeath to my church ten million dollars on his death. Emille and I decided we had to deal with him anyways, so it was to be a nice surprise. Six million to you and Emille, and four million for Carl and I, but Jake had to screw it up by killing two of Sarge's men and Emille."

Raul looked at Chadfee and said, "You dumb shit. You put a two-hundred-million-dollar deal in jeopardy for ten million and then screwed things up like this. Now with Emille dead, what kind of idiots are you?" Raul continued, "You come to me with a plan to use your remote school as a distribution center for my product. Emille said you had thought things out very well and that he liked the plan. I wanted him to run things for me here in the Midwest and then my whole empire, so I went along with your plans. Now here I am in this godforsaken Wisconsin cold and snow, six trucks worth of product, and my best men with me all at risk all because of your petty greed!"

Raul looked up at the ceiling where Dean had and said, "The dumb-ass pastor says you can see and hear us. I assume you can talk also. If so, for your own good, please answer me. I warn you, I am not a patient man!"

Jake thought a moment, looked at Cammie, and said, "I guess it can't hurt to see what he says."

Cammie answered, "Your call, Jake."

Jake pushed the talk button, saying, "I'm here, Vortez."

Raul replied, "Good, Mr. O'Nell. First, I want you to know I'm a very rich, powerful, and dangerous man. People do not screw with me. I have ways of making people pay for their sins against me and my family. Second, I do not think you are this drunken janitor that these idiots thought you were. I think you are a man, as we would say in our country, with large cojones. But now, you see, we have a problem here. You killed my nephew, Emille, and I have no sons. He was to be my heir to the throne. This means I am honor-bound to have you killed blood for blood."

Jake interrupted Raul saying, "Listen, I'm a rich, dangerous man myself, only I didn't get my money by being a scumbag drug dealer, and as for your blood for blood, your man, Sarge, there had my father-in-law killed!"

"Ah yes, the old man," said Raul. "Paco told me of that, but I'm afraid that changes nothing, but I am a man of honor. If you and the woman surrender now, I promise you both a quick death. Or if you continue to kill even one more of my men, I will see to it personally that you both take a long painful time to die. So, Mr. O'Nell, what's it going to be? I grow weary of talking to the ceiling."

Jake paused before answering in a voice so cold, so calm, that Cammie was glad, very glad that Jake was on her side and not one of the men on the screen. Jake responded, "A generous offer, Raul, but you have no idea who you're dealing with. I will give you my offer. You and your men walk away now, leave your trucks, and the good pastor and his brother for me, or stay and die. I won't give you another chance."

It got quiet, really quiet, then Sarge burst out laughing with the others joining in. Even Raul smiled. Sarge yelled, "What are you, some kind of superhero or just nuts. Tell us, big talker!"

Jake answered, "Sarge, you ever been to Afghanistan?"

"Nope," replied Sarge. "Never had the pleasure. My gig was the Philippines, why?"

"Well, Sarge, if you had, maybe you'd have heard of a place called Wasari Valley."

Steve interrupted, "O'Nell, I was in Afghanistan. So you're him then?"

Jake answered, "Yeah, I am. It sounds like you know my story. Why don't you tell it to Mr. Vortez, then we'll decide on how this ends."

"Okay," Steve said, looking at Raul, who nodded. "It was like this" was all Cammie got to hear because Jake shut off the sound, jumped up, and said, "Cammie, we have to move and move now. I bought us about eight to ten minutes. With Dean knowing about this room, we can't stay here." He took the butt of the shotgun and smashed the consoles and the controls for the security gates. "Let's move, Cammie," Jake said as he started to the door. Jake led the way down the main hall across the big gym. When they got to the wrestling and small gym doors, Jake turned to Cammie and said, "Stay here. I'll be right back, so no matter what you hear, don't move."

Cammie said, "Okay," and Jake took off at a dead run around the corner and through the theater seats, stopping at what looked like an ordinary electric breaker box. It was an ordinary box on the outside, but Jake hit the hidden switches and swung it out and away, revealing the actual main panel for the whole school—including the main control for the security gates, beside which hung the real "master keys" to the gates. Once he threw the switch, Dean was going to be screwed.

Jake debated on leaving all the lights on or to turn them off. He decided to lock all the lights on and turn on the flashing lights along the halls and by the exits. The last thing he did was shut off the door cameras before hitting the gate switch and closing the panel.

Now, he thought to himself, *you bastards are going to find out how a trapped rat feels and why the Marines taught their men to have a plan B.* Jake knew this school like no one else, even old Bob, and they would have a tough job finding him and Cammie. Jake took off at a dead run back to Cammie as the gates started clanging down in front of each classroom door and every hundred feet along the halls. Jake had designed it to isolate threats and keep as many kids and teachers safe as possible.

As Cammie waited for Jake to return, she was wishing she could have heard all of Jake's story.

Chapter 7

Steve was saying, "Jake O'Nell was a marine sniper and a good one. He had thirty-plus kills to his credit. He was like a borderline crazy with a death wish, taking the worst possible missions. The Army called him and his spotter in to help back up a ranger team that was going into Wasari Valley, only one of a thousand like it in Afghanistan. Intel had a tip a big Taliban mullah was coming south with not many guards to start some ops against NATO forces, then run back to Pakistan to hide like they always do. So this twenty-man team is way down in the valley floor setting things up for an ambush. Jake and his spotter were the high-ground cover, and as usual, the intel was bad. Jake and his spotter go around a bend, and not fifty yards away is this mullah and six of his men. They didn't spot Jake because they were looking into the valley, but O'Nell could see Taliban hidden everywhere below them. The whole thing was a trap. O'Nell doesn't hesitate. He charges in with his spotter, and they take out the guards with silenced .22 Mags and knives. The spotter takes a knife in the left leg, and within three minutes, the guards were all dead and the mullah taken prisoner.

"Jake tries to get the guys down below on the radio because he could see about half the guys are in the kill zone. He couldn't get a response from them, but the base had heard Jake, and this idiot colonel orders Jake to start back with the mullah. He would send help for the rangers. Jake said, 'No fucking way, Sir.' First, he drops a couple shots at our guys feet, making them head to cover, just ahead of the Taliban opening up on them. Then Jake takes and drags his spotter back behind them about forty yards, shoots the mullah in both knees so he can't run away, then rigs a Claymore mine to this guy's chest

28

with a pull cord to his spotter, telling him, 'If they get me, blow this bastard up and get out.'

"Then Jake goes to work on the Taliban below him. It seems this mullah had picked the best spot in the whole valley to watch from. O'Nell was able to pick the Taliban off with his .50 caliber as fast as he could shoot and load. It didn't take the Taliban long to figure out where they were dying from or wondering what happened to their mullah. So they forgot about the rangers and started up after Jake. By the time they get to the top, there's only five or six left. O'Nell finishes up with his knife on the last ones because he was out of ammo. They figured his kills at between forty to fifty. He was shot in the shoulder, leg, with numerous cuts and bruises, one eye swollen shut." Steve laughed afterward and said, "To get the mullah to talk, all they had to do was to show him Jake's picture. Then the best part, they get back to base, and the colonel jumps Jake for disobeying orders, shit like that. O'Nell doesn't even answer, just shuffles up to that colonel and lays him out cold with one punch. Then the Marines had a problem—Jake had saved twenty rangers, but had punched out a colonel. To top it off, the Taliban put a two-million-dollar bounty on Jake's head. So they promoted him, gave him some medals, and sent him home. He resigned and disappeared. That's all I know."

No one said anything for a moment. Then Raul turns to Rink and Dean, yelling, "This man is your drunken bum? That's what you told my Emille. What a couple of—" That's as far as he got because lights started flashing, and the security gates started coming down. Pastor Dean yelled, "Sergeant Michael, get to the maintenance room! O'Nell must have another key!"

Sarge yelled, "Let's move!" He, Steve, and three of Raul's men shot out of the office, but the first gate was halfway down already as they got to it. Sarge, Steve, and two of Raul's men made it, but the third did not. He had slid only a small way through the gate as it came down on him, crushing him to death. Raul, Paco, and Raul's two bodyguards came out of the office, trying to go outside, but they were too late!

Sarge yelled back up the hall, "Dean, you idiot! I thought you said O'Nell couldn't close these gates?"

Dean and Raul came closer to Sarge's gate. Dean said, "I don't know how he did it. There's only supposed to be one key."

Sarge said, "Raul, Sir, what do you want us to do? These are tough gates. We've enough C4 to blow maybe three gates. It looks like two gates before I can get to the control room, or should we get you outside?"

"No, Sarge, you get to that room. Get these gates up, find O'Nell, and kill him. You and your men get a million each if you can do it in an hour or less!"

Sarge and the men went to the next gate. Sarge told Steve, "Blow a hole in that damn thing, and after O'Nell's dead, I am going to kill me a preacher!"

Chapter 8

When Jake got back to Cammie, she asked, "What did you do?"

Jake answered, "I played an ace that Pastor Dean didn't know I had—I put the school in lockdown. It'll buy us a lot more time. So basically, I locked the bad guys in with us!"

"You what!" shrieked Cammie. "Are you crazy?"

"Maybe a little bit. It seemed like a good idea. Now come on in here." Jake led her into the wrestling room that doubled as a small gym. He didn't have to open any gates into these rooms because he'd seen no real reason to have gates, considering they had glass walls to the hallway that could be shot through, and there were gates all along the other halls. Jake had had to open one to get to Cammie again. Once inside, Jake said, "Give me one of your shoes." Cammie did, watching and wondering what he was up to as Jake went over by the big return vent for the AC. First, he took off the lock, threw it in the garbage, then used her shoe to put a small scuff mark on the floor by it.

Jake handed Cammie her shoe back and said, "I hate these things. You ever try to clean off the marks? They are a bitch! Now," he continued, "we hide in here." He crossed the room and pulled off a mesh cover from one of the three huge rollers that rolled up the wrestling mats.

"Last year," he said, "I found one of the seniors using this as a napping spot. He was a good kid, so I didn't rat him out. Now I'm real glad I didn't." He helped Cammie into the drum, and she said to Jake, "It's going to be snug in here."

Jake replied, "Slide down as far as you can." She did, then Jake slid in, pulling the cover back on as he did so. The shotgun muzzle pointed out. He left it just in reach as he slid down next to Cammie. Jake said, "If they do come in, I'm hoping they check the vent first. That way, I can get the drop on them."

"You mean kill them before they kill you," Cammie stated.

"Well, yeah, you can say it that way too. So anyways, I then grab their weapons, fight any more that come along, and you stay here! No matter what, snug as a little bug in a rug!"

"What did you say?" Cammie asked with surprise in her voice.

"Sorry," Jake said, "just a corny old saying I used to tell my kids."

"No, it's okay," Cammie said. "I heard it myself a long time ago. Do you think the sheriff will ever come?"

Jake answered, "Yeah, soon, Cammie." Then he thought to himself, *Goddamn it, Connor, where the hell are you?*

Chapter 9

After the line went dead, Connor had slammed his fist down on the table, causing the beer cans on it to jump. He was a big man, six foot two, and still in good shape for a man going on sixty. He'd been sheriff now for thirty years, one of the longest terms in the state.

A man in his late seventies came back over to the table and said, "I take it that was Jake."

"Yeah," said Connor, "and I think he was drunk as a skunk, the way he was talking. Something about some trouble at the school. Christ, he said Bob was dead and that he had killed three bad asses to save that Cammila Martinez woman. I'll nail his ass good if he's drunk at school and done something stupid."

The older man, Caleb Johnson, Connor's uncle and Jake's godfather, pushed the beer aside he'd been about to open and said, "Listen, Connor, first, as a favor to me, send a deputy to the school, okay? Then try calling Bob's cell, his home phone, and the school."

"Jesus, Caleb," Connor said, "you're not buying into Jake's crap, are you?"

Caleb said, taking Connor's freshly opened beer from him, "Just shut up and do as I ask. Then you and I are going to have a good long talk." Connor hadn't seen Caleb this upset in years, so he did as he was asked.

First, he used his radio and called into it, "Mason, you out there?"

Mason Peevy was his officer on duty tonight. A good young man, he'd been working for Connor for five years now. "Yeah, I'm here, Sheriff, just finishing up a traffic stop by Stone Brook Road."

"Okay," said Connor. "When you get done there, head by the Wineca High School. Jake O'Nell just called and said there's some trouble up there. Might be something, might not, okay."

"You got it, Sheriff. Car 618 out." Then Mason called, "Car 618 to dispatch. Mae, you there?"

Mae answered, "Where else would I be?"

"Hey," Mason said. "Just checking in, okay. The sheriff asked me to swing by the school, check on Jake, then I'll be in." He asked, "We still on for tonight?"

Mae replied, "We are if you're here when my shift is done, so don't be too long, and be careful. For some reason, it looks like Jake's got all the lights on at the school."

Mason came back with "Okay, I will. Car 618 out."

Chapter 10

Mason thought to himself as he headed to the school, *Yep, this will be a night Mae won't forget.* Mason planned to ask her to marry him. It turned out Mason was right. It was a night that neither would forget, but not for the reason Mason was thinking.

As he approached the school some twenty minutes later, he was still thinking about the best way to propose. Should he go down on one knee right away or wait until after dinner? As Mason turned down the school's drive, fifty yards down, he saw a black SUV sitting sideways, partially blocking the road. The driver's door was open with a guy dressed in dark clothes lying on the ground. Mason would always wonder if he had not been thinking so hard about his date with Mae, would he have reacted better to the whole situation? Starting with hitting the distress button on the radio before getting out, but he didn't. Nor did he call Mae. He ran to check the man on the ground. As he started to roll him over, the guy spun over and pointed a pistol at Mason's face, saying, "Don't move, Mr. Deputy." Then he yelled, "Come out, Harry, I got him." He then took Mason's gun he said, "I want to thank you, Mr. Deputy, for making me an easy hundred bucks. I bet Harry here you'd fall for it."

Then a second man walked up carrying a rifle and said, "Yeah, thanks, Deputy. I bet ol' Stan here you'd go to your radio before getting out or back away before checking on him. Had you done either, you would be dead now, and I would have a hundred dollars coming!

Chapter 11

As soon as Connor had signed off with Mason, he'd tried to make the calls as Caleb had asked, but got no answers anywhere. "Okay, Caleb," Connor said. "There's no answer from Bob's phone's or the school, but that doesn't mean Jake's call was legit. I'm sure Mason will come up with nothing, okay? We should hear from him in twenty to thirty minutes."

"Okay," Caleb said. "But while we wait, I'm going to tell you some things you should have known a long time ago, but I promised Jake I'd keep quiet. You know this being an uncle and godfather to you both besides, is a bitch sometimes. I tried not to take sides, but with me having to raise Jake and you his cousin always being here growing up, I was lucky and thought of you both as sons. With that said, I'll ask you this, Connor, in all the years since the day you were baptized, have I lied to you?"

Connor answered, "Well, there was that time on Shawn's Ridge when you shot at this 'monster buck,' and it turned out to be a spike, and that time on Oak Creek when we were fishing trout."

"Okay, okay, smart ass," broke in Caleb. "I mean, about the serious shit, stuff that really matters for Christ's sake!"

"Okay, lighten up, old boy," Connor said. "No more joking." Connor realized Caleb was really upset, so he added, "You're right, you've never lied to me, so tell me already what in the hell you're talking about."

Caleb sat down and said, "Okay, here goes. First off, Jake's not a drunk. He hasn't been on a toot since the one-year anniversary of the accident when he took out the stop light. In fact, that was only the second time in his life when he was actually drunk. The first time was at your bachelor party, remember? What a time that was!"

"Listen, Caleb, I remember, okay, and I know what you want, Jake and I back together as friends, one big happy family again. But there's things you don't know, like the fact he buys two cases of wine every week. Don't tell me anyone can drink that much wine and not be a drunk!"

Caleb started to laugh, saying, "Yeah, I know all about the wine. Jake buys it for the local churches that use wine and for the nursing homes for their residents' weekly happy hour." Caleb went on, "So that's why you tried to nail him last year, and his blood test came back clean as a newborn babe, didn't it? Connor, you're damn lucky that feisty lawyer Jake has didn't sue you and the county again. After the last time you tangled with that lawyer, I can't believe you tried to pull something like that."

"Okay," said Connor. "I screwed up, and you're right. I thought, sure, Jake would sue, but not a peep."

"Well," Caleb said, "Jake and his lawyer talked things over and decided to pay you back in other ways that would really piss you off."

Now Caleb had Connor's full attention as he asked, "And just what ways would that be!"

"Okay," said Caleb, "we have to back up some so it'll all make sense to you. When Jake got back from Afghanistan, he'd changed, finally coming to grips about the accident—at least a little, anyways."

"Hold on a second," interrupted Connor, "tell me about that. Did he get kicked out for screwing up?"

"Yes and no," said Caleb. "Jake was a genuine hero. He saved a bunch of our guys and caught this big mucky-muck mullah guy. Jake got wounded pretty bad doing it. Afterwards, this asshole colonel gets on Jake about not obeying his orders. Well, Jake wounded and all, punches his lights out. So the Marines gave him a bunch of medals and asked him to resign!"

Connor said, "Sounds just like Jake, but the thing I've always wondered is why Jake went back in, in the first place. After winning the lawsuit, he was set for life."

"I know," said Caleb. "I asked him that very same question. He gave me this BS about 911 and doing his duty. But I could see it in his eyes. He never planned on coming back. He was going so he could be with Korrine and the kids, but whatever happened over there, it changed his mind. He'd decided to live again, a little anyways. He still won't talk to me about the accident or the war. The only reason I know this much is because I managed to pry it out of Jake's lawyer, Mr. Jonathan Wayne Key. You know him, of course."

Connor said, "I'll never forget that bastard. The way he picked me apart at the trial. Anyways, Jake came back a tarnished hero who's rich." Connor looked at Caleb and added, "But I'm starting to think there's more to it than that, and I'm not going to like it am I?"

"You're right on both counts. You are so not going to like this story. Now where was I? Oh yeah, when Jake got back, he was in for a huge surprise. Before he left, he divided up the settlement money. He gave part of his money to his lawyer, part to a friend in Vegas, and part to me. He made us all full partners, told us to make it grow or lose it. At that point, he really didn't care what happened to the money. He honestly believed he was never coming back. His two friends took it to heart because he'd saved both their lives. They felt they had a debt to pay, and remember, we're getting half the profits too. I didn't do a lot, bought a few farms, as you know, raised a lot of corn, soybeans, and beef. Jake and I, on this farming deal, are worth about three million. Which I thought was pretty good, but Jake's two friends were amazing. They turned their cash from Jake, in twelve years, into 350 million for Jake's share—"

Connor interrupted Caleb, saying, "First, Jake's crazy call, and now this story from you. If anybody else was telling me this, I'd be taking them to the nuthouse!"

Caleb said hotly, "Just let me finish! The name of Jake's company is SSBBKO Enterprises. The lawyer came up with it. He thought it might help Jake. It stands for Shane, Shiloh, Brandon, Bridget, and Korrine O'Nell."

"Christ," said Connor, "SSBBKO Enterprises, you can't be serious?" He paused a moment, lost in thought, then said, "Jake owns the bank and, hell, just about everything else in this corner of the state. Jake's payback, my new house loan, all the hoops I had to jump through and the delays. That was all Jake's doing, wasn't it?"

"Yeah, you figured it out pretty quick, but there's more—and keep in mind you brought most of this on yourself, jumping to conclusions about him so fast. Don't get me wrong, Jake could have explained some things to you too, but you're both so damn stubborn, mules have nothing on you two! Don't forget all the good stuff he's done. New churches for that Pastor Dean and the Lutheran and Baptists. He gives tons of money to a Catholic bishop friend of his. He put up two new factories in the county, got the logging industry going again, hell, he even built your new jail."

"Okay," said Connor, "I get the picture, he's a fricking saint! But you tell me right now what else did Jake do for 'payback' as you called it. You want me to believe this bullshit, then I want it all."

Caleb continued, "All right, you asked for it. For starters, he was the one who put up the money for Toby to run against you last year in the election."

"But why?" asked Connor. "Jake had to know there was no way Toby Gent could beat me. I mean, he's a good guy and all, but the way he gets loud about things. Plus, he drives that big old hog of a diesel truck that's so loud and smoky, people hate it. I would have thought Jake could have backed a better choice!"

"But you see," said Caleb, "that was the whole point. Jake thinks you're a hell of a sheriff. He picked somebody that couldn't win. He paid Toby well, giving him a hundred thousand dollars in cash, plus a lifetime lease to Toby Jr. on the McTaw farm, and Jake paid all the election expenses. Toby had the time of his life. At first, he wouldn't do it until he knew why, and the why was to keep you tied up campaigning in October."

"Shit," said Connor. "The elk hunt. He ran Toby to keep me from going on the elk hunt with you and Benny."

"Bingo," Caleb said. "You're pretty bright when you want to be. You see, you thought it was just the three of us going, but Jake and your son, Benny, put things right between them a few months after Jake was back. Jake had wound up owning a company that built wheelchairs and stuff. He figured who better to run it than Benny and Bob's son, Curly, two people in wheelchairs themselves. It was a perfect match. Their company is a world leader in the handicapped field helping people work, play, and be a part of society again. Jake's pretty proud of them, so he, Benny, and Curly came up with the elk hunt idea. We figured it would be great, the trip you and Benny always dreamed of and the chance to put the family back together.

"Then you had to screw it all up by having Jake arrested and put in jail on bogus charges. What, pray tell, were you thinking that day?"

Connor answered, "I was having a shitty day, and I was just coming back from the graveyard. Somebody had busted up a bunch of headstones, and Hazel's was one of them. So I spot Jake coming out of the liquor store with all that wine. I had him grabbed that evening, going through the work of a Breathalyzer, which didn't read anything. I figured a blood test would show positive. We had it drawn but couldn't get results until the next morning, so I had to keep him overnight. What made me even more mad was the fact Jake never said a word, just looked at me like I was a piece of crap. So yeah, I screwed up. I was shocked when, the next morning, his lawyer shows up with a court order for his release. Jake still says not a word. His lawyer looks at me and says, 'Sheriff, sometimes you are such a dumb-ass.' That was one hell of a day.

"After Jake and his lawyer leave, I find out I have an inmate who says he fell and was in the hospital. My chief jailer gone, just a letter that said he wouldn't be back and that he quit. Plus, the surveillance tape was missing. Any chance Jake had something to do with that mess, that you'd like to share with me?"

"All right," said Caleb, "I'm coming clean, so I might as well clear that up too. You see, your jailer, Lem, and that inmate— Haskins was his name, right?" Caleb went on without waiting for a reply. "They tried to do a number on Jake, give him a 'life' lesson, Lem called it. They had no idea who they were dealing with. Jake busted them both up pretty bad. Then he calls Mason and Mae in to help him, and me too. Jake proceeds to explain to Lem and Haskins how he could make their lives a living hell, or they could have a second chance when they got out of the hospital. Lem took it. He's doing great as a foreman at the wood plant. He thinks Jake walks on water. That Haskins, he was an asshole. He told Jake to kiss off. Jake took no pity on him. He had him taken to Viking City and had his lawyer, the honorable Mr. Key, explain what would happen if he ever came back to Wineca or opened his mouth about that night. Plus, he was warned about ever trying to hurt someone again. Mr. Key has the missing tape, and Jake makes it a point to check in on Haskins now and then. He's actually doing well also. I guess sometimes fear can change people to the good. Anyways, Jake waited back in his cell, mad as hell at you, plotting his revenge."

"Caleb, I know I screwed up and pissed Jake off, but how did he get Mason and Mae to help him? A bribe, I suppose?"

"Nothing like you're thinking. Mae's folks were about to lose their bar and house. Jake bought them and leases them back to them for a hundred dollars a year and upkeep. He did the same thing for Mason's sister. She was losing her house after her husband died, plus he gave her a hundred thousand dollars so she could raise her two kids and only have to work part-time. Mason and Mae would have done anything Jake asked, including jail time. To them, he was already a saint."

"Some Saint," Connor said, "taking the law into his own hands and all the rest for revenge. Christ, it must have cost him three to four hundred thousand dollars."

"Closer to six hundred thousand, and I don't agree about how he handled everything, but you broke his shell for the first time in all those years. Jake finally showed some real emotion and coming back into the real world again. He was talking to ghosts way more than was good for anyone. The elk hunt was a blast. He was our old Jake again. I even had Tana come as a surprise for everyone!"

"No frickin' way!" shouted Connor. "She swore to never have anything to do with Jake again. How the hell did you manage that?"

"It wasn't as hard as you think. You see, she lost her husband four years ago in Afghanistan, and Jake found out, so he arranged for Benny to accidently check on her. Benny wound up squealing on Jake, how he'd been helping her secretly for a long time, money-wise.

I know Benny and Tana will kill me for this, but the time for secrets is over, don't you think?"

Connor nodded his head saying, "Go on, tell me the rest."

"Benny and Tana are getting married, and you and Jake are going to be grandpas. Tana's due in six months. They want you and Jake to knock off all this BS and put this family back together again. The plan was for all of us to get together Sunday, right here, hash things out once and for all. You don't know how hard it has been watching you and Jake butt heads and not saying anything because I love you both." Caleb was choking up as he said it.

Connor quietly said, "Caleb, I love and respect you. You've always been there for me, and I have to admit, some things make more sense if what you say is true. But before I can believe all this, answer me this. If Jake is as rich as you say he is, why does he drive that old junk Ford truck, live in a mobile home, and work at the school for nine dollars an hour?"

"Bob gave that truck to Jake and Korrine for a wedding present, and he's living where he and Korrine first did. So, Connor, why do you think he lives there and walks those lonely halls night after night? You of all people should be able to figure it out. You've been there yourself, for Christ's sake!"

Connor was very quiet for a moment then spoke in a soft voice, "He won't let go. Their memories are haunting him. Every day, he sees the kids in the halls and Korrine sitting on the bench, so real you can almost reach out and touch them, but when you try to, poof, they're gone. Yeah, I was there when Hazel died. If it hadn't been for Benny, I might still be there."

Caleb continued. "Now Jake only had me, a grumpy old man, but he had that school. He put his heart and soul into it. Secretly, of course, making it green as they say nowadays, with in floor heat powered by a wood boiler, using our most renewable resources along with solar panels, geothermal heat, plus building it three times bigger than was needed for the future. Jake also added a state-of-the-art security system. You've done a walk-through with your deputies, so you know about the door cameras with the monitor in the principal's office, and the principal can lock outside doors as needed, plus photo FOBs, etc. But what you don't know about is the secret security room Jake had put in. There's cameras covering the whole school and parking lot, controls for security gates hidden in the ceilings, and even a small arsenal to fight back. Jake is determined there will be no Columbine here. That's why we kept it a secret from you. We figured you'd be against the guns."

"I used to be until the way the world has changed. The terrorists are here, and I think we should have police officers with guns in all the schools. Israel does it, so do fifty other countries. They realize how important our kids' lives are. The US government can pay for all this bullshit around the world, but won't pay to protect our kids! Now I wish Jake could have told me more on the phone. He might have been serious!"

"Holy shit!" Caleb yelled, jumping up. "I totally forgot about Jake's call. I got so wrapped up in storytelling. I'm getting old. What exactly did Jake say?"

"Jake told me Bob was dead, and he killed three bad guys that had kidnapped Cammila Martinez. Oh yeah, one even more weird thing is he said to tell you 'Alamo,' and then the phone went dead."

"Man oh man!" yelled Caleb, more upset than Connor had ever seen him before. He went on yelling, "We've been sitting here like two old senile farts yakking, and Jake's in trouble—bad trouble! Only Bob, Jake, myself, and Pastor Dean know about the room, and we take turns on manning the cameras. We came up with a few code words to save time or if somebody was in a bind. Alamo means a 10-33, 'deep shit and call in the law' situation. Connor, Mason must be there by now. I'll grab my rifle and ammo from the safe."

"I'm on it," said Connor, the sheriff in him coming to full alert as he thumbed for his radio calling, "Car 618, you there? This is the sheriff. Come back, Car 618, you there!"

Chapter 12

Stan and Harry had been trying to decide what to do about Mason, thinking things must not have been going as planned in the school. They'd done as they'd been told, hide down the main highway for two hours then come in and guard the driveway, nobody in or out. They had a police ban radio to monitor the law channels, and they'd been told that someone would come and give them a status update or new orders. Stan said, "This sucks that Sarge can't use the damn cell phone. No service this day and age? Talk about hillbilly land." Harry answered, "You got that right, but what do you make of those explosions we heard and what might have been gunshots?"

"You got me. With all the guys back there, they should have had no trouble. Still, I—" was all he got to say because right then, Connor's page came through the radio. "Okay," said Harry, putting his gun barrel against Mason's head, telling Mason, "You answer that call and be real careful with what you say. One wrong word and you're dead. Got it?"

Mason nodded his head and answered the radio, "Yeah, Sheriff, I'm here."

"What's your twenty? Are you at the school?" Connor asked.

"Yeah, I saw Jake, and he seems fine. Bob cut an electric line, and it shorted the phones out."

"Okay, I guess that's it then. Where you headed next?"

"I was thinking of going down to Travis Crossing, see if I can catch that Lennie Basil kid. You know, the one with the big ears. He'll be off work soon, and maybe I'll nail his speeding ass tonight," Mason answered with a slight laugh.

Connor paused a second then said, "Sounds good, go get him, over and out."

Connor grabbed Caleb's landline phone, Caleb asking, "Did you catch that part about Lennie Basil?"

Connor hissed at him, "Shush a second, will ya," thinking, *Come on, come on* as the phone rang on, wishing Mae would answer the phone, and she did on the second ring with "Hey, Caleb, what's up?"

"Mae, it's Connor. Listen to me. I'm calling from Caleb's house. Did you just hear Mason and me on the radio?"

"I did, and I was just about to call Mason and ask him what he was trying to pull!"

"I figured you'd do that. Thank God I got you before you did. I knew you would catch that part about the Basil kid. Anyways, I think Jake's call for help was real and he was in trouble and now I think Mason is too!"

"Oh no!"

"Stay sharp, Mae, okay! This is what we're going to do first. I'm calling Mason back, and you listen only, no matter what you hear. *Do not* reply, got it?"

"Got it."

"Second, I want you to use the landline or cell phone only. Call Harlan at the State Patrol. Tell him our radios are being monitored. Have him call up as much help as he possibly can—officers in need of assistance. He is to standby. We'll let him know the situation in forty-five minutes. If you don't hear from us in forty-five minutes, Mae, it'll be on you. I want all the help you can get our guys, SWAT, EMTs, MedFlight. After you call Harlan, you get Butch and the posse in. Call Larry and his firefighters, but no alarms. Remember, Mae, make them understand phones only. No radios, no sirens. Mason's life might depend on it."

"Okay," Mae responded, trying to hide the emotion in her voice. "No word from you in forty-five minutes, I get them rolling!"

Connor came back softly saying, "You hang in there. Mason's a good cop. He's used his head to warn us. Now you make those calls. Just listen and stay strong."

After he hung up, Caleb said, "I guess you did catch that part about the Basil kid."

Connor barked back, "Hey, give me some credit, old boy. We all know Lennie's been in Basic Training for six months now. I bet you didn't catch that part about the big ears—that's our code for the radios are being monitored."

"Not bad," Caleb said with a big grin.

"You ready to go?" Connor barked. "The second I'm off this radio, we're going to that school!"

Connor said into his radio, "Car 618, one last thing."

Connor breathed a sigh of relief when Mason replied, after getting a go-ahead nod from Harry, "What's up, Sheriff?"

"Nothing big, kid. Now that Mae's off for the night, I just wanted to ask you if the rumors true, that you're going to propose to her tonight? Is there any truth to it?"

"I don't know how you know about that, but yeah, I was going to pop the question tonight after my shift."

"No shit! Are you sure about this, I mean she's nice and all, but she's more than a little on the heavy side. It'll take most of your pay just to keep her fed."

Mason responded hotly, "Very funny, Sheriff, Sir, but that's my fiancée you're talking about, and you're one to talk. You're no lightweight."

Chuckling, the sheriff responded, "Calm down, kid. Hell, my late wife was a big gal, and we had twenty-six great years together. I was just ribbing you. Good luck, I hope she says yes. This sheriff is going to bed. Over and out."

Harry and Stan were laughing like crazy. Stan said, "Lawman here's got a fat girlfriend."

"Yeah," said Harry, "sounds like she's a ton of fun." They laughed even harder.

This was the moment Mason had been waiting for. He knew the sheriff was aware he was in trouble because everybody knew Mae was lucky to weigh a hundred pounds soaking wet. There was no way he was going to the school with these jokers and be used as a hostage. It was twenty yards to the pines alongside the road to the school.

Mason knew if he could get to them, Harry and Stan would have one hell of a time finding him, even with the snow. He knew how ugly and thick it was in there because he and Jake rabbit-hunted in there. Mason bolted for it, and he was fast, catching Harry and Stan so off guard they both missed their first two shots. But then, Mason's luck ran out. On their third and last chance before he made the pines, Stan's shotgun pellets caught Mason in the back of his head and neck, and Harry's rifle drilled him square in the back.

Mason dropped eight yards short of his goal, not moving as the world went black around him. He could still hear Stan and Harry laughing, but all he could see was his Mae's face, as bright as ever, even in the darkness that settled around him.

Chapter 13

"Jake," asked Cammie after they were snuggled in, "can I ask you, how long have you had your room with the cameras and stuff?"

"Since the first day the school was opened, and I know what you're going to ask. You're going to ask about November twentieth two years ago."

"How," she gasped. "How did you know that?"

"First, November twentieth is the day the world stopped for me. I lost most of my family in an auto accident, and second, what Rink did to you that night has haunted me for over two years. You know I was ready to come forward and nail that bastard, Rink, for raping you, but you never said a boo. No call to the sheriff, then coming in on Monday morning like nothing had happened. It didn't make sense. I was thinking of taking the tape to Connor, but then I thought on it awhile, and I figured you had your reasons. So I waited for answers that never came. Now look, had I come forward, Rink would be in jail, and maybe none of this happens and Bob would still be alive."

"Maybe you're right, but I'll make you a deal. I'll tell you my whole sad tale, give you those answers you want, and you can decide if I should have come forward. But if I do, you have to agree to do the same. After all the shit that's gone on here today, I want to know who the real Jake O'Nell is, because he's not this clown he wanted the world to see. Is it a deal?"

Jake thought for a moment before he answered, "Why not? I guess I owe you that much, so go ahead, your tale first, Cammie."

"First," she said, "my story won't take long to tell. The reason I didn't report Rink for raping me is because I'm here illegally. I snuck into the US from Peru. I live with my aunt and pretend to be her daughter. She is a US citizen, so I used her social security number to get into college and then get this job. My father was a professor at a university in Lima. My mother was his assistant. I was an only child and led a pretty sheltered life. We weren't poor, nor rich. Happy is what my dad said. I had sixteen wonderful years, and then"—Cammie paused a moment—"and then on my sixteenth birthday, there was a terrorist bombing in the market. My parents had gone to the market to get me a cake and presents. Twenty-one dead, which included both my parents. So I was forced to live with the only relatives I had in Peru. An uncle-in-law—my mother's sister had been married to him until her death two years before. His name was Hector, and he was a gross pig. I would have left Peru somehow right away if not for one thing. Hector had a daughter from his first marriage. Her name was Nikki. She was a year older than I. She was so pretty, and Nikki knew what kind of man her father was, and she kept me safe from him. Nikki and I became close and then, like it was meant to be, we became lovers."

Cammie continued, "Even with Hector always watching me, trying to catch me naked or alone, it was the most wonderful fifteen months of my life. We were soul mates. We made plans to escape Hector the day I turned eighteen. Our dream was to be together forever.

"Then with two weeks to go before my birthday, we became careless. The beast, Hector, caught us together. He went berserk. He knocked Nikki out and raped me, yelling that I was for men to be used, not women, shit like that! By the time he was done with me, Nikki had come to. She told Hector that he was an animal and that we were leaving. Hector grabbed her and choked her to death, all the while looking at me and laughing. He said to me, 'Now look what you've done. You'll spend the rest of your life in jail for killing my poor Nikki.' He laughed again. I snapped. I knew even though he was a monster, that in Peru, I would be found guilty on his word alone. So I grabbed Nikki's scissors that she used to cut my hair with, and stabbed him as hard as I could. First in his groin, then when he fell screaming, I stabbed him many times in his throat. He would rape no woman ever again. Then I lay there crying with Nikki's head on my lap for hours, waiting for the police to come and take me to jail. They never came. I searched and took all the money I could find in the house. I was lucky Hector had much hidden away, enough to get me to the USA and to my aunt. Before I left, I gave my Nikki one last kiss and used the scissor to cut some locks of her hair. I still have the locks of her hair and the scissors!

"Anyways, after I got my degree, we came here to Wisconsin, living in Portman. It's a long drive every day to work, but it keeps people from asking questions or getting too close. I thought I had found peace here, then Rink raped me. I wanted him to pay, but I couldn't risk going back to Peru. I was so scared of that Monday morning wondering how Rink would be, knowing I hadn't called the cops on him. He leered at me that day, but you had work to do on my rooms, and we started eating lunch together. Then Rink was gone for three weeks. When he came back, it was like he was scared of me. I never had a problem with him again, until today. I even thought it was because of the fact you were always around when he was near me. Or I would dream a little that you had something to do with the change in Rink after his time off. So I kinda thought of you as a hero before today. Pretty silly, huh?" Cammie finished up with "Well, that's my life story up to today!"

Jake had listened quietly as Cammie told her story. It had touched him deeply. He had guessed some of it, but now to hear her soft mellow voice in his ear with the semi-darkness around them, his heart that he'd thought was long dead was coming alive once again.

Jake chuckled and said, "No, Cammie, that's not silly, not silly at all."

Cammie replied, her voice full of hurt, "Tell me, Mr. O'Nell, what is so funny? I tell you my story, things not even my aunt knows about, and you're laughing at me!"

Jake answered quickly, "Cammie, calm that Spanish temper of yours down. Your story moved me deeply, and I ache for what you went through. Thank you for sharing it with me. What I was laughing at was about Rink changing his ways. You guessed right about me having something to do with that. So should I just skip to the part about Rink, or do you still want to hear my story of woe?" At that very moment, they heard a dull explosion and, faintly, several gunshots.

Cammie hugged Jake tightly, and Jake began to stroke her long black hair. He whispered softy, "They're trying to get through the gates. We'll hear more soon, but we're okay here."

"If you think we're safe, then yes, tell me your story, no short-cuts. A deal's a deal."

Jake thought to himself, *Why not?* Maybe it was time to tell someone alive what he'd gone through. He'd only told the Army's shrinks and Caleb what they wanted to hear.

Chapter 14

"Okay, you asked for it. I too was an only child, like yourself. My parents were wonderful. We had a farm on Hillview Ridge just a short ways from my uncle Caleb's farm. He's a confirmed bachelor, and he's also godfather to both Connor and me. I had lots of cousins. We fished, played, hunted, and of course worked hard together on our farms. Even though he was two years older than I, Connor and I became best friends. Things couldn't have been better. We didn't have a lot of money, but we were rich with family and friends.

"Then the year I turned fifteen, my mom got cancer. She only lived two months past my birthday. Six months later, my father killed himself. It was a shock to everyone, but me, I'd seen it coming. On the day of my mom's funeral with just the two of us left standing by her grave, he said to me, 'I love you, son, but without her, there is nothing in this world for me.' The day of mom's funeral is the day I remember losing both my parents. The only reason Dad waited six months to kill himself was so I could collect on a large insurance policy he'd taken out for me. So I moved in with Caleb, my guardian.

"I grew six inches in the next two years, becoming a star in baseball, football, and basketball. I was the man! The big shot everybody both loved and hated, but wanted to be. When I was a senior, I went to Hillview then, we came here to play the Wineca Hounds in a basketball game. We were killing them. They had no way to stop me, but this little guy kept pressing and pressing until I had enough, and I knocked his ass to the ground, right in front of the Wineca cheerleaders. The little guy had hit his head, knocking him out cold. All of a sudden, this little spit of a cheerleader, runs out and kicks me as hard as she could in the shin—*bam!*—then the other. I go down and am lying there, shins on fire, looking up at her as she keeps yelling at me. I look up at her thinking she's as cute as a bug's ear. Her face all flushed, fists clenched, glaring down at me, I lost my heart to her on the spot. I never really believed all that stuff about love at first sight, figured it was all bullshit, until that moment.

"Well, by then, all hell was breaking loose, and I don't get a chance to see her again the rest of the night. The next morning, I could still see that face. I couldn't get it out of my mind. It took me a few days to find out the guy I knocked out was her brother. Curly was his name. He was a hunter and fisherman, same as me, and we became hunting friends. Oh, it took a few weeks, but I finally managed to get a date with her, my dream gal. Korrine was her name, and that first date was a disaster," Jake said with a chuckle. "If Curly and I hadn't become such good friends, that night might have been the end of Korrine and me. But I hung in there, and she finally fell for me. From then on, over the next six months, we were inseparable.

"Then two weeks before I was to leave to play football for Wisconsin in Madison, she comes to me and tells me we're going to have a baby. I acted like a total asshole. Yelling at her like it was all her fault. She didn't even cry or yell, just walked out with her head held high. That was worse than if she'd have thrown a fit at me.

"Anyways, that night, I got a midnight visitor. You see, old Bob Haley was her dad. I woke up with him standing over me with this big ol' ten-gauge shotgun, cold and the size of a cannon, stuck in my privates. I was terrified. I couldn't move or speak. Bob looks at me and says, 'Son, we have a situation here.' Bob being Bob, he got right to the point, saying to me, 'You have three options, Mr. Big Shot. One, you stay here and marry my little girl, get a job, and take care of her and the baby. Option two, you marry her and join the Marines. Maybe they can make a man out of you, if you can pull off your four-year hitch. By then, Korrine will be out of school, and if at that time you don't want to stay married, I won't stand in your way to get a divorce. Option three,' he says as he clicks off the safety, 'I pull this trigger, and you can go ahead, take off for college, only as a changed man who doesn't have to worry about getting any other gals pregnant. You have one minute to decide!'

"It took me eleven seconds to say I'll take option number 2. To me, it looked like the best way to escape the mess I was in.

"'Good,' Bob replied. 'I kinda hoped you'd pick that option, but 3, that one would have worked out too!'

"Korrine and I got married the next morning by our county judge, and I was signed up and in the Marines by five that evening. Five days later, I was at boot camp in Georgia, a long, long way from playing football in Wisconsin. It turned out okay though. Curly signed up when I did, and we wound up in the same unit.

"There really wasn't any named wars going on right then, but we did a bunch of hush-hush stuff in Bosnia, the Philippines, and places like that. It was way different than now. If our boys get in trouble now while fighting these Islamic terrorist bastards, they call for help. Back then, since we weren't supposed to be there, we were on our own. Most of the time if we ran into more trouble than we could handle, they'd try to come in and get us out of there as quick as possible, but sometimes it wasn't so quick.

"We ran into that situation in a godforsaken little hellhole in Africa. Of the forty of us that went in, by noon the next day, there were only twenty of us who weren't dead or seriously wounded. I found out what real men are made of, including myself. Curly was seriously wounded and had lost a leg. When the choppers came, those of us not wounded or badly wounded, made sure every single body and wounded comrade got on the choppers first. I carried Curly out to the choppers. Just as we reached them, the bastards hit us one more time. This time, I got hit. I took three slugs and shrapnel from a mortar, causing serious enough wounds that I was allowed out early. I only had two months to go, but I was ready to be a husband and a father.

"Old Bob was so happy I saved Curly he got me a job with him at the school, and I took it. I ran our farm during the day, worked four nights a week at the school, and took classes two nights a week to get a teaching degree in history and one in coaching. As soon as I got my degrees, I quit the farming and custodian work, because during this time, Korrine and I fell completely and hopelessly in love. Then the kids started coming. Our first was Tana, a beautiful girl. It took her a while to get used to me after being gone most of the first four years of her life. But finally, she did, then we had twin boys, Shane and Shiloh, and next was Brandon. Somewhat later, and the last was little Bridget. Things couldn't have been better.

"That is until November 2000. I was head coach of our football team. The best team Wineca ever had. Our twins, Shane and Shiloh, were seniors, Connor's son, Benny, was our senior quarterback. Brandon was a sophomore. Things started going wrong. With only two weeks left in the season, Benny was caught drinking. I had to bench him according to the rules, a three-game suspension. So our son Brandon started at quarterback. He was terrific. We won the next three games, and we had one more to go. If we won that game, we would play for the state championship at Camp Randall in Madison, the first time ever for Wineca High School. The day before that game, Benny comes to me in my office asking if he was starting again the next day. I was so full of myself back then I thought I knew it all. I guess to this day, I don't know why, but I told him no, that he would have to sit the bench. Brandon would start. He gets mad, throws his jacket, and I hear glass break. I picked up the jacket and find pieces of glass from a small bottle of booze in the pocket. Benny never said a word, but took his jacket and walked out.

"Brandon started the game but got hurt on the second play. My only other quarterback was a freshman, and we ended up losing the game. His dad, hell, the entire team and everybody asked where Benny was. I just told them that we'd had words and that he didn't show up. If I had told anyone about the booze bottle, Benny would've been suspended and not been able to graduate with his class. I thought I was doing the right thing, but it wound up costing me everything.

"In the locker room after the game, my boys and I got in a huge fight. They decided to ride home with Korrine. She asked me, 'What the heck is going on?' I told her we'd talk about it when I got home. She was mad clear through, but all she said was 'Okay, fine.' Those were the last words she ever said to me.

"You see, Benny had been drinking since he left my office and was just driving around. Connor had stopped him shortly after the game and just told him to go home. Conner admitted later in court that he knew Benny had been drinking. Benny didn't go home as he was told though, he wound up on River Hill Road. We'd gotten two inches of snow after the game, and the county hadn't plowed or sanded the roads yet. It turns out that all the plowmen had gone to the game and figured on doing them as soon as the game was over. Benny lost control on the hill and plowed into my wife's van, causing it to roll down an embankment and into the river. Tana was off at college, but Korrine and the four kids were gone, all gone."

Jake stopped for a moment and looked off into the darkness. "I'm so sorry, Jake," whispered Cammie. "I had no idea. I mean, I heard about the crash, but no details. You can stop if you want."

"No, it feels good to finally talk about it, Cammie, and then you'll be the only one who knows all my secrets. That way, if I don't make it today, I know I'll have somebody that can tell my sad story."

"Okay, finish your story, but don't even kid about you not making it. I believe God had you save me today, and he'll protect us, you'll see!"

"God? That's a nice thought, but I stopped believing that fairy tale kind of shit a long time ago. Things just happen." Jake went on, "So anyways, Benny lived but lost the use of his legs. Tana came home and took charge of everything. The days leading up to the funerals, the funerals, all that was a huge blur.

"It was a Sunday, the day after the funerals, and I somehow wound up here sitting at my desk in the coaches office. That's where Tana found me. She looked at me and said, 'I heard what happened after the game. You know it's your fault that they're gone, don't you!' I started to explain, but she wouldn't have any part of it, wouldn't listen at all. Just told me, 'Stay away from me—as far as I'm concerned, you're dead too!' Then she was gone.

"I don't remember how I got through that night, and the next day was worse. I went to see Benny in the hospital, and he told me to drop dead. To make matters worse, as I was leaving, I ran into Connor. He starts yelling, blaming me, and telling me about how all this is my goddamn fault and to stay away from Benny.

"I went home to a cold, empty house, looking at all the memories that hung on the walls. Pictures of hunting, fishing trips, proms, vacations—it was all there. I sat down and wrote out my will, got my pistol, grabbed a couple of beers, and was about ready to join the rest of my family when there's a knock at the door. In walks Curly on his crutches. He had another marine buddy of ours with him, Jon Wayne Key. I'd saved his life twice while we served together. They asked if I had a beer for them too, neither saying a word about the gun in my hand. You see, Curly called Jon right away and told him how I was hurting and how everyone was blaming me. It turns out Jon was a lawyer, and a damn good one. Jon says to me, 'Thought you might want to know a couple things Curly and I found out about the last couple of days.' He went on to tell me about Connor not taking Benny's keys and how the county hadn't plowed the roads and how the state had ordered that a guard rail system be put along the river road. How the county had paid for it to be done, but the contractor, a big-shot construction guy in town, had decided to wait a year to do it because he had taken on too much and couldn't get to it that year.

"Jon said to me, 'Jake, you see, it's not your fault! If you decide to, we can make them pay.' Curly added, 'Think on it Jake.'

"They finished their beers and walked out, me still holding my gun. I sat there for over an hour or so, then I got mad, real mad. I put my gun away and called Attorney Key. I told him to go to it, and he did. When it was all over, I had won the lawsuits, putting ten million in the bank. It was a hollow victory; they all hated me around here. Tana still refused to talk to me, so I rejoined the Marines.

"It was just after 911 when I rejoined. Before I left, I had Jon put a million dollars into a trust account for Tana, gave a million to Caleb Johnson, my godfather and told him to farm like he always wanted to and dreamed of. Gave seven million to Jon, my lawyer, and told him to start a company and see if he could make it grow, and the last million to another Army buddy of mine that lived in Vegas. He'd always bragged when we served together how, if he just had some seed money, he could make some real money in that town. So I gave him the money and told him the same thing, make it grow.

"I became a sniper, volunteering for every suicide mission I could. You see, I never planned on coming back, so first it was Iraq then Afghanistan. In the first six years, I lost three spotters and had six wounded. Nobody would go with me unless they were ordered to. Then one day, this young marine comes up to me, with the brightest red hair you ever saw. He says to me, 'My name is John Henry Teach, and I want to be your spotter.' I looked the kid in the eye and asked him, 'Do you know what you're in for?'

"'I do,' he answers. 'Word is, you're a dead man walking, same as I am.'

"'You're pretty young to talk like that.' So I asked him, 'What's the catch?'

"The young marine paused before answering, 'I lost my wife and parents in a fire. We'd only been married four months. They were all the family I had, no brothers or sisters.'

"'Okay, kid, you're in.' We spent the next five and a half years taking out the bad guys wherever they sent us. Then came Wasari Valley. It was rough. I disobeyed orders to save twenty Army Rangers, some of America's finest. John Henry and I were both hurt bad. So while we're lying there waiting for our ride out, hurting like hell, John Henry looks at me and says, 'Sarge, my wife had a cousin about my age. She lost her husband a couple years ago. My sister-in-law says she keeps asking about me. She's a real-looker, Sir, and funny. If it's all right with you, Sir, I think that it's time for me to give this shit up. I don't want to die anymore, Sarge, I just want to go home!' I looked at him and all around us and started to laugh, really laugh. For the first time in all those years, I was laughing. I turned to him and said, 'Mr. Teach, I think it's time that I go home too, and if you don't look that gal up and marry her, I'll kick your ass.'

"Turns out the Marines were glad to get rid of me too. They promoted me to Captain, gave me some medals and an honorable discharge. I came back home, first to Vegas, looked up my partner, L. J. Monty is his name, to see how long it took him to lose my money. But as it turns out, L. J. was sharp and knew what he was doing. We owned a half dozen businesses, worth around fifty million and growing."

"Oh, you really are rich, Jake," Cammie said.

"You haven't heard the good part yet. My lawyer friend, Jon Key, turned that seven million into a 250-million-dollar company. Caleb did real well too with land and cattle, worth about three million on the farm end of things in Wineca County."

"Jake, of all the things that's happened today, this is the hardest to believe. I mean, they say you drink hard and live in an old trailer home on a rundown farm, and of all things, you work here in your own school for nine dollars an hour for goodness sake."

"Yeah, well, first off, I'm no drunk," Jake stated sternly. "A cold beer once in a while because, once again, God's wisdom comes through. He made an Irishman who loves beer, but made him allergic to hops. And as far as where I live, it's no dump. It's all I need right now until I figure out what's next for me. You see, when I found out how stinking rich I was, I had no idea what to do with it. Then Caleb tells me that the state is condemning the old school here, forcing Wineca to join with Haleysville. It was just the idiots in Madison's way of trying to get rid of another little school. So I agreed to build this new school, but do it right. In-floor heat run by a wood boiler, making this whole school green before I'd even heard the term. A complete fresh air system—sickness is down 40 percent from the old school. Plus, I made it big enough to handle three times as many kids as we have now, and I kept as much as I could of the old school.

"Then I looked around and saw how this whole area was hurting. I started a company based in Wineca to build schools like this around the country plus the new lumber mills and other companies. Our buddy out there, Pastor Dean, finds out about my money, talks me into building him a new church, which I did, but I did the same for the Baptists and Lutherans. I did donate a great deal to the Methodists and Catholic churches also. I don't believe in God, but if I'm wrong, those churches do a lot of good, and it might help me out with the Big Guy. Like I said, if I'm wrong.

"Then somewhere along the line, I even got the idea of playing God myself. I was going to right the world's wrongs. I started with a teacher here by the name of Lori Blue. They called her Coach Blue. She taught English and coached boys' basketball. One of the first women coaches in the state to coach boys' basketball, and she was a damn good coach. Then one year, she decides to bench a senior player to start her son, who is only a freshman. The senior takes it hard and commits suicide. His older brother, everyone, including myself, thought it was from what Coach Blue had done. His older brother and I decided to make her pay, and I had the ways and money to do it. We had a gal come in as a student and claim Coach Blue seduced her. We doctored up some photos and got her fired. Her husband left her and got custody of their three kids. We were all feeling so smug and righteous about what we had done.

"Then this kid's brother finds a hidden laptop with pictures his brother had taken of himself abusing the neighbors four- and six-year-old children. There was also a note that said he thought he was near to being found out and that if he was caught, he would kill himself before going to jail, as he knew that in his heart he was evil. So," Jake continued with guilt in his voice, "Coach Blue was innocent all along. I guess I was so quick to judge her because of what happened with Benny and me. I went all out to make things right with the coach and her family. It cost me a bundle, but worth every penny of it, and they're doing well. That's when I decided to stop trying to right all the world's wrongs. I help people when I can, and I've only bent the law twice since. Once as payback to Connor for locking me up on bogus charges, and the second was two years ago to right a wrong that happened on November twentieth that year."

Cammie gasped, "The day Rink raped me. Jake, what did you do?"

"I'll tell you, and you'll see why I laughed when you asked me if I had anything to do with Rink staying away from you. Like I said, I waited for you to come forward. When you didn't, I figured you had your reasons. I respected your choice and kept quiet, but no way was I letting him get away with it. I knew his type. It was only a matter of time before he would go after you again and again. So I arranged for him to win a weekend in Las Vegas plus get five thousand dollars spending money. He took the bait, just like I knew he would. I called on two of my marine brothers to pay Mr. Rink a little visit. They were more than happy to do it when they found out why. In fact, they offered to make him 'disappear' for good. I told them, 'No, just make him suffer and live with the guilt.' They paid him a midnight visit.

"They tied Rink to the bed naked and gagged him, ransacked the room to make it look like a big party had happened. Then they took a box cutter and made nineteen cuts to his penis, one for each minute he raped you. They told him you were being watched over, and they would come back if he ever touched you again. They finished up with a call to 911 from one of their girlfriends. She told them where Rink was and how it was a wild party that Rink had wanted, but it got out of control with his wishes of being cut. The cops came, got Rink to a hospital. He tried to tell them what happened, but they wouldn't believe him. After all, it was Vegas." Jake finished with "Well, that's my story, and I hope you can forgive me for taking the law into my own hands and laughing about it."

Cammie was quiet for a moment, then she started to laugh, saying, "Forgive you nothing, that's the sweetest thing anyone's ever done for me" and laughed even harder. She said, "I prayed for God to punish Rink somehow, and he'd already gotten a taste of hell. Can you just picture that weasel trying to tell the cops his story and them trying not to laugh? He must have hurt like hell. No wonder he took three weeks off and why he walked so funny. He told everybody he had a groin pull. *Ha!* How many stitches did he have to get, Jake?"

"Sixty-two," Jake answered, trying to muffle his laugh.

Cammie started giggling again. "Oh, Jake," Cammie whispered as she kissed him on the mouth with a long, hard kiss. Jake didn't know what to do for a second, becoming lost in the moment until Cammie asked softly, "I hope that was okay." Jake answered her with a long, hard kiss of his own. Cammie asked softly, "Jake? I know this is going to sound insane, but would you make love to me?"

"Now that would be nuts. You do remember that there's a bunch of bad guys trying to find us and kill us?"

"I know, but hear me out. I never really made love with a good man. I've only been raped twice by animals. If we do die today, I want to know what it is to be loved by a man with the kindest heart in the whole world."

Then she said, "You do too, because I don't think that's a shot-gun barrel I feel against my leg, is it? And that's not a doorknob you've got a hold of, is it?" Jake laughed, realizing he had been squeezing Cammie's breast softly.

"No, it's sure not a doorknob." Jake thought, *Why the hell not?* "Okay, Cammie, but it's been a long time since I've made love."

"Hell, it's been a lifetime for me," Cammie answered with a laugh as she kissed him again softly. They made love quietly and urgently as they knew they must. Much to Jake's surprise, he did remember the right buttons to push. The passion was exquisite. When they finished and were lying there in each other's arms, spent, Cammie softly whispered to Jake, "Now I see what the fuss is all about. I can see where a girl could get used to that and long for it. Jake? Did I do okay, and is it like that all the time?"

"Well," Jake replied teasingly, "for someone who thought they only liked girls, you were okay, and yes, that's the way it can be if two people love and care about each other, or even better."

Another explosion came, this time really close. Cammie said, "Jake—" but before she could go on, Jake blurted, "Shit, that's the last gate before the hall to us. Two rooms to check, and they'll be in here." Jake and Cammie fumbled their clothes on, Jake stopping before sliding up to the shotgun and getting ready. "Cammie, um." He hesitated then went on. "If we get through this, could I, well" he said, stammering again before becoming quiet.

"Mr. O'Nell, are you asking me for a date?"

With a laugh, Jake answered, "I am, but I just wasn't sure how to go about it after we just, well, you know!"

"Jake, I'd be honored to go anytime, anyplace with you."

"Cammie, there's a special place I want you to see on our farm. I know this will sound like a stupid first date, but this place, we call it Gordie's Rock, named after my great uncle who found it. There's a bench carved into the solid rock, by whom, no one knows. It was already there when Uncle Gordie found it. From that bench, you can see our family's whole valley. When the sun rises, it makes the entire valley glow with golden magic. A hundred yards directly below is a spring-fed pond. Not big around, only about three acres or so, but it's deep and clear. We fish for trout there, and when the sun reflects off it, it is beyond beautiful. All the fathers in our family take their sons or daughters there for their first hunt, making a memory bond that lasts forever.

"I sat there with Korrine, then Tana, then the twins. The year of the accident was going to be Brandon's turn on the rock, and Bridget was going to come with to bring good luck to him. Bridget, she loved all the boys, but there was a special bond between those two. I know this might sound cold, but as much as I would give to hold either one of them again, that's the only thing I thank that God of yours for, is that they were together when the cold brutal water took them." Jake had to pause a moment before he could continue, then he went on so softy that Cammie could barely hear him say, "That's the date I want to take you on, a picnic lunch and just sit with me. I'm not asking you to hunt with me, just sit. It was Korrine's favorite place."

"Oh God, Jake, it sounds incredible, but are you sure you want me there? It's such a special spot to you."

"I do. If you can just sit there with me and understand even a little of that place, then you can understand a big part of me. It's the only place that makes me think that this God of yours is even a possibility."

"Jake O'Nell, I would love to go see this Gordie's Rock of yours. Maybe I'll even hunt. I used to hunt with my Papa."

Now it was Jake's turn to be surprised, asking, "What the hell do you hunt in Peru, llama?"

"No, you dummy, we hunted Andean geese and quail. I loved it! Papa and I had so much fun. We'd bring them home to Mama, and she would fix them up so good to eat. It was so long ago. It seems like only a faraway dream now."

Jake quickly put his hand over her mouth, whispering, "Shh, not a sound" into her ear. She nodded, and Jake slid up and away from her, grabbing hold of the shotgun, waiting, just out of sight. They'd heard one of Raul's men say as they came into the gym, "Look at that vent, Sarge. That looks like the best spot so far."

Sarge turned to his man, Steve, and asked, "What do you think?" Steve swung the vent door open and said, "Looks like a good chance.

There's a fresh heel mark here, and these screws have just been taken out. I'll bet this thing's got branches and hidey-holes throughout the whole school. This would be perfect now that preacher man ratted out O'Nell's security room. So I guess the only question is, who goes in first?"

Steve turned to look at Raul's men; both of them shook their heads and backed away. Sarge said, "Looks like you got the job, Steve."

Steve looked into the vent and said, "Okay, Sarge, on two conditions. First, if I get nailed in there, you promise to get my money to my wife and kids?"

"Yeah," answered Sarge, "that I can do. What's the second?"

"You and those two," Steve said as he pointed to Raul's men, "have to put your safeties on your frickin' guns. I can take the thought of O'Nell shooting me in the face, but no damn way can I stand the thought of one of you getting jumpy and shooting me in the ass. If I didn't die, I'd never live it down!"

Sarge and Raul's men started to laugh, switching their safeties on, with Sarge saying, "Okay, kid, go get him."

"Thanks, Sarge," Steve mumbled, turning as if to go into the vent.

Jake had been listening and edging ever closer to the end of the tube, thinking his long shot might just work. He was hoping they'd all go in or leave, at the most, one man back. He planned on jumping out, using the element of surprise to nail the bastards from behind, then deal with the rest. He hoped for the best—as his mom used to say. *Although,* Jake thought to himself, *Mom probably wouldn't have thought of applying it to a gun battle.*

Jake would never know if his plan would have worked or not.

Chapter 15

What happened next caught him off guard, to say the least. It was a fatal surprise to Sarge and Raul's men, for as Steve turned as if to go into the vent, he whirled back around, firing his automatic rifle at Sarge. His first two shots caught Sarge in the throat, knocking him to the ground, and he was dead instantly. Taking no chances with Sarge being the most dangerous of the three men, he shot him again in the forehead before turning to fire at Raul's men. Steve killed the first of Raul's men before the man could even get his gun up. The second man reacted quicker! He and Steve fired at the same time. Steve hit the man three times dead center, mortally wounding him. Steve was shot in the thigh and right shoulder, forcing him to drop his rifle. He knew he was done as he watched the second man's rifle barrel pointed at him point-blank. He could only watch as the man's finger tightened on the trigger. Then it was Steve's turn to be amazed as he heard the roar of a shotgun blasting his foe back three feet.

Jake fired twice more, putting the man down for good. Jake then turned the gun on Steve. "Whoa! Don't shoot, Captain O'Nell!" Steve yelled as he slumped up against the wall, his one good arm in the air. "I'm on your side."

"Okay, son. First your name then your story, and lastly, how did you figure we weren't in the vent?" Jake asked.

"The last one's easy," Steve replied. "When I took that quick look down the vent, I could see there weren't any tracks in the dust, so I took a chance that you were close by and made my move. My name is Steve Garvey, Sir. I was an Army Ranger, one of the men you saved in Wasari Valley. I've been waiting a long time to try and repay you back for saving my life, and now I owe you again. Minos there, the guy you finished, had me dead to rights."

Jake put the gun down, saying, "I'll be damned. You can put your arm down, soldier, and I think you got this one wrong. Mr. Garvey, it's you who saved me, plus one more."

Steve glanced over to see Cammie crawl sheepishly out of the tube. "Hi, Mr. Garvey. Call me Cammie."

Jake turned back to Steve asking, "Okay, Steve, how bad you hurt, and do you have a mess kit?"

"I took one in the shoulder. It didn't go through, so it's not bleeding much. The one in my thigh here went through clean, no bone, but it's draining me pretty good. Sarge has a good med kit on him."

Jake proceeded to patch Steve up, giving him a double shot of painkiller while asking him, "How did you get mixed up in this bunch, and what is going on here?"

"I'll tell you," Steve said, "then we'll use your plan to get away, Captain? I mean, you do have a plan, don't you, Sir?"

"Well, first off, it's not sir or captain anymore, just Jake. Second, to tell you the truth, I hadn't planned too far ahead. I thought that if I couldn't keep us hid, I'd make a break for it, get Cammie to the woods, taking as many of your friends out as I could along the way. Basically, I figured I'd more than likely be dead by now, but with Sarge over there dead and you being able to tell me what we're up against, we have options. So tell me your story, and let me think on a plan."

"You wanted to know how I got hooked up with Sarge—stupidity and need would be the best two words to describe it. I just got out of the Army six months ago. I'd planned on staying in until I could get my pension, but my wife said it was time for me to get out and spend more time with her and our four boys. I agreed, thinking it wouldn't be that hard to get a good job and finally buy a house. But I couldn't get a good job anywhere, and we were barely making it. Then three months ago, I ran into Sarge over there. He offered me a job for what he called 'security' work. The pay was fantastic, and my family needed the money. I knew that Sarge had been dishonorably discharged, but I agreed to work for him, and it was stupid. By the time I found out who I was really working for, it was too late.

"Once you join Raul's 'family,' as he called it, you're in for life. Raul's nephew was the enforcer of that policy. Jake, you did the world a big favor getting rid of that son of a bitch."

Jake gave Cammie his "I told you so" look with her grinning back and sticking her tongue out. Steve forced himself to sit back up before continuing, "I figured the day was coming when I would have to try and kill all three of them, Raul, Sarge, and Emille. It would have been my only way out. If even one lived, they would come after me and my family and friends. Emille used to brag about how Raul had been betrayed by a police captain in a little town in Mexico. They went in and killed half the town, the captain's family, his horses, and even the man's dog just to send the message that you don't betray the Vortezes, and they waited four years to do it! That's the part that scared me the most. No matter how long it took, they would come, so keep that in mind as you think on a plan, Captain Jake. Raul has to die today somehow!

"Last, what we're up against. Raul's up front with Paco, his number-1 man and about three others; the preacher, his weasel-faced brother, and then there's a guard or two at each door. Out back, there's six semitrailer trucks loaded with dope of every kind. This school, with all those extra rooms, was going to be a central warehouse once the old man and you were gone. Rink was going to get Raul's men in to replace you. Then there's at least three or more guys in each truck."

Just then, they heard faint gunshots coming from the front offices. "Jake," Cammie said, "maybe that's your cousin, the sheriff."

Steve started shaking his head. "I doubt it, Ms. Cammie. Raul has his two best men guarding the road into this place. They have everything, RPGs, M18s, and nobody is getting in that way without one hell of a fight and a lot of noise. My bet is Raul just dissolved his partnership with those two assholes, Dean and Rink."

"Well, maybe you're right," Jake replied, "We'll find that out sometime, but right now, we have to come up with that plan you wanted. My first thought was for the three of us to bust out an exit door to get to the law."

Steve interrupted, "Sorry to stop you, Sir, but if you and the lady want to go, I wouldn't blame you. I'll go back and try to kill Raul, but remember he is a cold-blooded bastard. He will keep coming after you no matter the cost."

Jake cleared his throat. "Like I started to say was that, that was my first thought, to run. But number 1, I've not much on running from a fight, and number 2, I agree Raul has to be taken out for our future safety. That and I want some payback for my father-in-law, Bob. Number 3, I can't just let Connor walk into a trap. Those two have to go on the road. So this is how we'll do it. Raul will be my job. We've got some firepower to work with, thanks to you, Steve. Your job will be to take Cammie out of here, either pick off those two up front or get to the main road and warn the sheriff about them."

Steve thought for a second before answering, "The Raul part I agree with, you know this school, and I think you can do it. But I think my best chance would be to go alone. I might be able to catch them off guard. Let's just put Ms. Cammie back in your hiding spot. When the bullets start flying, she'll be safest in there."

Jake looked at Cammie. "What Steve says makes sense, Cammie, but it's your call."

She looked at Jake and nodded, saying, "Okay, you two. I know when a girl's not wanted, so I'll stay. But you two had better not forget me. Can you leave me the shotgun, if there's any shells in it?"

Jake checked it. "It has two, Cammie." She slid into the tube with Jake's help, and he slid the shotgun in beside her. Jake leaned in and asked her, "How about a kiss for luck?"

She gave him a good hard kiss. Then she looked at Steve and said, "Good luck to you too, Mr. Garvey." She blew him a kiss as she slid out of sight. "When you come back, don't sneak up on me. I'd hate to shoot you by mistake." She was laughing as she said it.

"Thanks, Cammie," Steve said as he and Jake went out the door. "That's quite a gal you got there, Jake. You been together long?"

Jake looked at the clock before answering, "Yeah, she's something, and we've been a couple now for about two hours."

Steve wanted to ask another question, but he had to hurry to keep up with Jake. They went through the gate that Steve had blasted open for Sarge. Jake led Steve across the big gym through the theater until they reached the stage entrance door. Wineca's school had a unique theater setup with a stage both inside and outside. People loved to sit outside in movable bleachers and chairs for plays or concerts when the weather permitted. Jake had opened three gates to get to the small door. He turned to Steve. "Steve, this goes out onto the outside stage. There's three sets of steps off the stage, center, left, and right."

"Yeah, I remember seeing the layout when I went around the school. Sarge has two men by the center steps. Oh shit! I almost forgot. Do not try to use the AC doors to go out. Sarge had me rig that door to blow if you tried to sneak out."

Jake looked at him and stated, "That's a good thing to know. I'm glad you remembered that. Now a couple things, first, here's a couple of my business cards. If you run into the sheriff, his name is Connor Hess. He might be with our uncle, Caleb Johnson. You show them one of these cards. You tell Connor that you work for me, and I had you come in because I suspected Rink. Have Cammie back up your story on that, I know she will. Then you call my lawyer and partner, Jon Wayne Key. Tell him Jake said to call you Little John, you can trust him completely. He'll take care of you and Cammie."

"Okay, got it," Steve answered. "What else?"

"Well, we need to take care of the guards out there. You go get your Stan and Harry then wait for the law. If I don't come to you by then, you come through here. Caleb has a key you can use or blast the knob off, but you get to Cammie and get her safe. I'll leave the gates up so you can get to her quick. I'm going to go kill me a drug lord. One last thing, Steve, if we get out of this, you've got a job for life. You'll have to move here to Wineca. It's not a big city, but you can get a house or a little farm. We've got lots of hunting, fishing, and good people. We could use a man like you around here."

Steve looked at Jake. "God must have decided to smile on me today. My family would love it here. I love to fish, and my wife is a huge hunter. We've talked about things that you just described, a place of our own with a garden, chickens." Steve was quiet for a moment then stuck his hand out and, with obvious emotion, said, "I would be honored to take your offer." Jake shook Steve's hand, and Steve stood back and saluted Jake, telling him, "Thank you, Captain, luck to you." Jake returned the salute and then slowly opened the door. He and Steve were both ready to fire, but to their surprise, no one was there.

Steve said, "See, Captain Jake, God is looking out for us, like having me remember about that booby trap. He knew it wouldn't have looked good for me to blow up my boss the first day on the job." He grinned.

Jake smiled and said, "You and Cammie are so going to get along. Now go!" Steve was left wondering to himself what Jake meant by that last comment.

Jake watched until Steve was out of sight among the school vehicles in the parking lot, then he slowly worked his way back to the main hall that led to the front offices. As he crossed the gym, he looked down the hall where Cammie was hidden, thinking to himself, *I hope I live to take her to Gordie's Rock like I promised.* Then he cussed himself saying, "Knock it off, old man. Just do the job like you always do—kill them all. Let St. Patrick sort them out." Jake thought one last thing to himself as he started again; he sure wished he knew if Raul and his bunch were caught in his trap yet. That would make things so easy.

Chapter 16

After Sarge and his group had left, Raul and those with him weren't sure what to do. Raul said to Paco, "Maybe I should have had Sarge free us with his explosives. I let my thirst for revenge blur my thoughts. I do not like being here like rats in a trap."

"Does anyone have a goddam idea how to get us out of here?" Now Raul was yelling, and he turned to face Dean and Rink, asking, "How about you two geniuses?" Both men were smart enough not to answer him.

Then one of Raul's bodyguards, Miguel, spoke up, "Sir, I think if I can get to the wiring, I can open the gates to the outside."

"Try it," Raul barked. "If you do, I'll give you a hundred-thou-sand-dollar bonus."

Miguel yelled, "I'll be shooting now," and he emptied his pistol into the Sheetrock wall, using the butt of his pistol to knock it out of the studs until he found numerous wires.

Dean had been waiting for a chance to talk to his brother with-out the others hearing him. He pulled him back into the far corner whispering to him, "Listen, Carl. I'm pretty sure that once that gate goes up, we're dead. I have a couple of Jake's pistols, so if you get a chance, run for it and hide. I'll keep them busy then come and find you, okay?" Carl Rink nodded his head slightly. He was scared to the breaking point, but he believed in his brother above all else, so he would be ready to do as Dean wanted, run and hide.

At the very same time that Rink and Dean were having their secret talk, another like it had been going on twenty-five feet away in the opposite corner. Raul told Paco, "I think it's time to get rid of these idiots and get the hell out of here. We send three trucks to Minnesota and three to Illinois. Do you agree?"

Paco replied, "I do, Sir, and that last gunfire we heard, I fear Sarge found O'Nell, and it did not turn out well for Sarge or our men." Raul thought to himself, *Perhaps we should have taken O'Nell's offer.* Then his anger returned, saying "no" to himself. "Raul Vortez runs from no man."

Carl Rink had been slowly working his way closer to the gate. He'd made up his mind that when it started up, he was going under it and out. No matter what, either way, this nightmare was going to end. He would either be out and free or dead.

Rink had never been much of a man to begin with, and after his Vegas "lesson," there was much less inside than before. Dean knew his brother well and had been watching him. Dean knew what his brother was going to do and said almost the same thing to himself; at this point, they had nothing to lose. But Dean had no intention of running; he had a different plan in mind.

Raul started to say to Paco, "Maybe, we have to have a little faith in Sarge—" But he never finished his thought because at that point, Miguel yelled, "I did it." As the gate slid up, Carl bolted, sliding under the gate and out the front doors. Paco yelled, "Get him!" While everyone's attention was on his brother, Dean made his move. He calmly walked up behind Raul and shot him twice in the back of the head. The Colt's .45 caliber bullets killed him instantly. As Raul's body hit the floor, Raul's men pointed their guns at Dean, but by now, Dean had his gun on Paco, just two inches in front of Paco's nose. Dean yelled, "Paco, tell them to put their guns down!"

Paco gave a little nod and said, "Do as he says."

"Now listen, Paco," Dean continued, "you're a smart guy. We can all start shooting and wind up dead, or you and me, we take over Raul's operation. With Emille dead, the world would have to answer to you. All I want is to run the Midwest operation for you. We'll blame Raul's death on O'Nell. It's perfect. It's your call. Do we start shooting and dying, or do you become top dog and rich?"

"We have a deal," Paco said as he pulled up his gun, shooting Miguel and the other bodyguard as he answered. Paco turned back to Dean. "Ricco here takes over my position if he agrees."

Ricco looked at all the bodies around him and quickly answered, "Si, Si, of course. And, Paco, you did right to shoot these two, they would have betrayed us."

Paco put his gun away. "Okay, Pastor," he said, "let's talk about what to do next."

"Okay," Dean replied as he to put his gun down. "First order of business is we have to get our trucks someplace safe."

"Agreed," Paco answered. "I know where to send them, and O'Nell, we make sure he dies. If not today, very soon—you got that, Dean? Now let's go around the school on the outside through the parking lots. I've a feeling it will be safe."

They picked up the men guarding the doors. They told them O'Nell had killed Emille, as they knew, and now had killed Raul and maybe Sarge, and that Paco was now in charge.

Had Jake and Steve been just two minutes sooner, there would have been a gun battle, but that is what luck or fate is, more often than not, a matter of timing. Sometimes good, sometimes bad!

Paco and Dean reached the loading dock to find they had a problem. The men had started to unload two of the trucks into the empty rooms, and when the security gates had come down, it had trapped half of the drugs from each of the two trucks in the school, along with all but six of Raul's men. One of the truck drivers had a small cutting torch and was using it to slowly cut through the gate bars. Paco went over to the man and said, "Hold up a minute will ya, Sam?" Then he yelled, "Listen up, everybody." The men gathered around Paco and Dean on both sides of the gate. Paco informed them, "O'Nell killed Raul, Emille, Miguel, and the others. As of right now, you will take orders from me. Pastor Dean will be in charge of the Midwest operations, and Ricco here is my number 1."

Then a big ex-marine with red hair, his name was Rueben but went by "Red," said, "What is this bullshit you're shoveling us? I thought all we had to deal with was an old man and a drunk?"

Paco answered, "Sorry, Red, I know you and Sarge were friends, but the drunk turned out to be an ex-marine sniper, and he's good, mighty good. So it's time to change things up here. Sam will finish cutting this gate open then we bug out. Red, if you will, I'd like you to be my number-2 man. Men, if you have any problems, you come see Ricco or Red. As of now, pay rates are doubled, and if we get these trucks out of here and to safety, it's doubled again. Any questions?"

Only one man spoke up, a hawk-faced man called Bruno. He said, "This sounds like extreme bullshit. How do we know Raul, Sarge, and Emille are really dead? And why is Paco and this here Pastor in charge?" Just as he finished speaking, Ricco shot him right between the eyes.

As Bruno dropped to the ground, Ricco said to the others, "It's true what Paco says. Raul told him to take over as he lay dying. I have been with Raul my whole life, so you know I speak the truth. So do we sit around fighting among ourselves, waiting for O'Nell to kill us too? Or do we work now for Paco and Pastor Dean making lots of money?" The remaining men looked around at one another, avoiding Bruno's body, nodding their heads yes.

"Good," said Paco, "let's get these bars open. Once we do, Red, you take your truck and Sanchez's and head north to St. Paul. Ricco, you take Pedro and head south, four men to a truck. Once Pastor Dean and the rest of us finish reloading these two trucks, I'll come south to Illinois. Dean will go north. Don't let anything short of the f'ing Army stop you." Just as he shouted his orders, they heard shooting from the main entrance.

Dean bellowed to Paco, "What the hell is that all about?"

Paco answered, "I think Stan and Harry gave some visitors a warm welcome, which means our time is running out. Red, blow those damn gates with an RPG, *NOW!*"

Chapter 17

Paco didn't know it, but Harry and Stan wouldn't be doing much of anything anymore. Steve had limped up to them, yelling, "Hey, guys, all hell's busted loose. Sarge and Emille are dead. This O'Nell bastard is a former macho marine, not some drunk custodian like we were told." Harry and Stan looked at each other, then Harry asked, "How'd you get away, and where's Raul? Did you leave him for O'Nell?"

Harry and Stan had survived by not trusting anybody or anything. Steve could see they weren't buying his story. They both had their fingers on their triggers ready to fire. Steve figured, for the second time today, he was a dead man. But he vowed to take both these sons of bitches with him. It was at that moment that Mason tried to crawl to the pines. He'd been awake for a while, hurting like hell, but still alive. He knew that if he made a sound or moved, Stan and Harry would have had fun finishing him off. So he played dead, praying for a chance. Finally, his chance came, only a slim one, but he had to take it. As Stan and Harry argued with this stranger, Mason struggled to get to his knees. Realizing he couldn't go up any farther, he started forward on his knees. As he tried to move, he let out a loud groan of pain. He couldn't help it, the pain was so intense, and his entire body was throbbing. His groan, which he thought for sure was going to cause the death of him, actually turned out to be a lifesaver for both him and Steve.

Hearing the groan, Stan and Harry turned to look at Mason. Harry said, "Looks like our deputy here has been playing possum." Harry died a second later as Steve used the distraction as his chance to bring his rifle up and firing, hitting Harry in the head. Stan died harder. He was quick and fired off a round, striking Steve in the left leg and knocking him down, but Stan had taken three rounds from Steve, all in the base of the throat. That was where Steve always aimed in case his enemy had a flak jacket or vest on.

Steve lay there a minute catching his breath. He knew he couldn't stay there on the road any longer; he had to move. The pain-killers from Jake were wearing off, and all three of his wounds were bleeding badly. As he forced himself up, using his rifle for support, he reached over and grabbed Stan and Harry's weapons. He hobbled over to Mason, dragged him to the tree line, and propped him up against a huge old pine then plopped down next to him. Mason looked at Steve and said, "Thanks for saving my life." Then he asked, "Just who the hell are you anyway?"

Steve stuck his hand out and said, "My name's Steve Garvey. I work for Jake O'Nell. You know him?"

Mason weakly took Steve's hand, answering, "Mason, Mason Peevy's my name. Hell yeah, I know Jake. He's a good friend of mine. They don't come any better than Jake O'Nell."

Steve murmured, "Shit, sounds like trouble coming." They could hear trucks coming up the road from the school. "Mason," Steve said, "there's a lot of bad men coming in them there trucks. We'd better let them go. Just play dead."

Mason answered, "That won't be hard with the shape I'm in." So both men lay there, not moving or shooting as four semitrucks rolled by.

Ricco didn't even slow his rig down, saying over the radio, "Looks like Stan and Harry ran into that damn O'Nell too! Christ, he must be something."

"You said it," answered Red. "I see a cop car there too. I'm glad we're getting the hell out of here." As the trucks each turned their separate ways, Red yelled to Ricco, "Next time I see you, drinks are on me."

"It's a deal," Ricco answered.

"Connor! Look out," Caleb yelled, just as Red and his partners pulled their rigs out of the school driveway. They were headed north toward Wineca and damn near ran Connor and Caleb over. Connor completed his turn, and the trucks roared by. "Jesus," Connor said through clenched teeth, "those bastards are lucky I can't chase them."

"Those trucks just don't make any sense," Caleb said. "Texas plates, dark glass, and roaring out of the school like that."

"I know" was all Connor got to say because all of a sudden, his lights revealed Mason's squad, and it was parked just a short distance from a dark SUV. "Shit," Connor spat out, "looks like there's bodies lying between them. Caleb, you loaded?"

"You bet. I'll cover you," Caleb answered as he jumped out and got ready, using the door as a rifle rest. Connor stepped out of the car. He drew his pistol moving ahead slowly shining his mag light back and forth, searching for trouble.

He heard a faint voice yell, "Over here by the trees, Sheriff. Don't shoot, your deputy's with me. We're hurt bad!" Connor moved toward the men, slowly telling Caleb to "Put the squad lights over here." Caleb turned the spotlight onto the tree line, revealing two men propped up against the trees.

Connor yelled, "Keep your hands up, whoever you are."

Steve yelled back, putting up one hand, "My name's Steve Garvey. I work for Jake O'Nell, and I can't put the other hand up—my shoulder's broke."

Connor approached the men slowly. He could see Mason was hurt and hurt bad, but Mason sat up a little and said, "It's okay, Sheriff. Steve here is one of us. He killed those two bastards over there that shot me up. He saved my life, Sheriff."

"Okay, Steve, was it? Put your hand down. Caleb, bring me the med kit," Connor said and turned back to Steve. "Now tell me, what the hell is going on here!"

Steve tried to sit up before answering, "Well, it's about drugs, lots of drugs, and they're Raul Vortez's. He's at the school yet with two more semis like the four that just left here. Two went south, and two are headed to the north. Vortez is working with Principal Rink. They were going to use the school as a distribution center, but Jake was on to them. He hired me to help try and nail them, but things got all screwed up. They killed old man Bob and took Cammie to use against Jake, but that only pissed him off more. He's got Cammie safe, and he's hunting them now. I got wounded inside, so Jake sent me out to warn you and kill those two if I could. Thanks to Mason here, I did." Steve went on, "Jake says you're a good sheriff. He said to tell you to stop those trucks and don't let Vortez escape. Those trucks have a lot of bad, bad men in them, and they have firepower. Warn your people. Make sure they know what they're up against."

Just then, they heard gunfire from the school. Steve grabbed Connor's arm and said, "Sheriff, Jake's taken out eight to ten of those bastards, but there's about thirty more. Please help him. He's the best guy I've ever known." Steve passed out and slumped over.

Caleb quickly asked, "Is he dead, Connor?"

"No," Connor answered, "but he's shot to shit."

"Connor," Mason whispered, fighting to stay conscious, "you and Caleb have to go help Jake. You can't do anything for Steve and me. We'll be okay till the EMTs get here. Help Jake, stop the drugs, tell Mae—" Mason passed out, not finishing his sentence.

Connor stood up and ran back to his squad, grabbing the radio and started yelling into it. "Mae, you there? What about Butch? Mae!" yelled Connor.

"We're here," Mae said. "I'm putting you on speaker."

"Listen up, Butch," Connor bellowed into the radio, "there are two big rigs coming your way, Texas plates and black tinted windows. The trucks are loaded with drugs. Each truck has about four to six men in them, and they are armed with heavy firepower and lots of it. Set up a roadblock by the four corners coming in on Highway 13. Use fire trucks, squads, whatever it takes. Get all the manpower you can, Butch, and make sure they're armed good. I want those trucks stopped if you can. I don't want anybody to die that doesn't have to, but we need those trucks stopped. You have about twenty minutes, got it? Now move!"

Butch was already heading out the door as he yelled back over his shoulder, "Got it." He ran across the street to the firehouse to line up the men and trucks.

Connor went on, "Harlan, did you copy that?"

"I did," Harlan said. "You want us to help Butch or come to you?"

"Neither," Connor said. "You've got two more rigs coming your way, North on 13. Get a hold of Leo to help. Same deal, Texas plates and black glass windows. Got it?"

"Got it, we'll shut them down. Luck to you, Connor," Harlan answered.

"Back at you, Harlan, be safe," Connor added before turning his conversation back to Mae. "Mae, you call us up some help, every damn thing you can. We have two officers down by the front driveway. Alive, but hurt bad. Send them out and tell them to look by my squad!"

"Oh, no, not Mason," cried Mae.

"Mae, listen to me, you hold yourself together! Yes, one's Mason, but you need to do your job right now! Okay, Mae," Connor said into the radio.

"Okay," Mae replied softly.

"Good. Now you pass the word we have Raul Vortez and a bunch of his men bottled up here with possible hostages and multiple casualties. We need MedFlights, EMTs, SWAT, and get the National Guard and wake the goddamn governor if ya have to."

"This is for you bastards in your big trucks. You heard me get things going so now you know the whole state will be waiting for you. We're not the hicks you take us for. If you don't give up, we will kick your asses!" Connor yelled into the radio.

Caleb turned to Connor, "We going in?"

"I am. I owe it to Jake," he answered.

Caleb put his hand on Connor's arm. "Hold up, sounds like trucks coming."

They stood listening as a truck started up the drive then gunfire rang out. Connor yelled to Caleb, "Let's turn these vehicles toward the school. Put the lights on bright."

"Oh, yeah. Give us a really good target to shoot at!" Caleb shouted as he jumped into the squad.

They just barely made it, getting the squads in place as a truck came roaring up just as more shots rang out. "I bet that's Jake," called Caleb. Then the truck was on them.

Steve had awoken at the sound of the gunfire and a roaring truck. He smiled and thought to himself, *That's it, Captain O'Nell, give em' hell!* as he passed out again.

Chapter 18

Jake, after leaving Cammie, had taken his time listening every few moments for any noises out of the norm. He'd also taken the time to kill the hall and main lights; shadows were his friends. As any custodian who works long, lonely nights in schools, businesses, or anywhere knows, when you're all alone, you get a feel and understanding of each creak and groan your building makes. The sounds that break the quiet that settles in once everyone else is gone, and you are all alone.

With only the emergency lighting on and the exit signs flashing, the whole school had a surreal feel to it, like something out of Dante's Inferno. Jake maneuvered his way through the school, approaching the main hallway. He could see that no one was ahead of him as he went through the last blown gate.

Jake knew the smell of death all too well and was not surprised to see bodies lying by the front entrance. As he opened the gate and rolled over the bodies, he was in for a huge surprise, not finding Rink and Dean, but Raul and two of his men. Jake smiled to himself, thinking, *Steve was right. The rats did have a falling out, and the little rats won.* He slowly went out the front doors. He took one last look at Raul, thinking, *Mr. Vortez looks like a big pile of dog shit more than the king he thought himself to be!*

Chapter 19

Carl Rink had decided things had been quiet long enough, that and he was freezing, so he was going to try and sneak back into the school and hide. As Rink came around the corner of the school to Jake's left, they saw each other at exactly the same time. Rink let out a whimper and turned to run back around the corner, just as two quick shots from Jake's rifle chipped the corner bricks, missing Rink by an inch at most. *Damn,* thought Jake to himself, *too slow. I should have nailed that SOB.*

Jake debated going after Rink, but only for a second, because he figured that if Rink was by himself, then Dean and the others must have gone around the back through the parking lots to their trucks in the back of the school. Jake made it around to the outdoor theater without seeing anyone else. He gave a sigh of relief, starting up the steps to go get Cammie. As he did, he heard a big rig start up, and it was coming his way, fast! Jake took cover behind Cammie's little smart car. He opened fire on the truck as it sped toward him, blowing out the windshield and wounding the driver. Paco leaned out the busted windshield firing, riddling Cammie's car with bullets. Jake got one shot off as the truck passed by, but it was enough. His shot struck Paco right in the heart. Jake emptied his clip into the truck, blowing out some tires and slowing it, but not stopping it.

"Shit, they got away too!" Jake cursed to himself. He started around the school again. He heard firing from the front entrance from two or maybe three guns. Jake said to himself, "'Bout time you got here, Connor!" That was all the time he had to think as Dean had sent four of the men around the corner to see what the shooting was all about. As soon as they spotted Jake, they opened fire, not taking time to aim. Again, Jake's years of training and combat paid off. He dove to the ground and returned fire, killing one man, hitting another, and forcing the other two back around the corner.

It was then that the semitruck came roaring back. Jake figured he might be done for, but once that truck had gone past Jake, it had tried the front entrance. The driver was blinded by the squad lights and already wounded when Connor and Caleb opened fire on him. He'd had enough and was turning the rig around when the other men in the truck yelled to him to turn around and go back. The driver was tough; he plowed on and turned the rig around, but not before catching another bullet from Caleb's old .30-06 rifle, killing him. He died hard, making it back to the middle of the parking lot where he smashed into Dean's SUV, bringing the truck to a stop but catching fire as it did so. With the fire setting off explosions of fuel and ammo, Jake knew he didn't have to worry about that truck anymore, or the men in it. But he stitched the corner of the building with slugs in case anyone was still there. When no return fire came, Jake went ahead, slowing to the corner. All he found was the body of the man he killed. He figured the others had gone all the way back to the loading docks, but he stayed on high alert.

Jake approached two trucks parked between him and the last corner before the loading docks. One truck was Bob's brand-new Ford, and the other was the school's maintenance truck. As he got even with the two trucks, he heard a shout from behind him. Jake hit the ground, bringing his rifle up to shoot, but he realized it was Connor and Caleb running toward him. Caleb shouted, "Don't shoot, you trigger-happy bastard! We're on your side!" When they got to Jake, he said, "You boys are lucky. You look as ugly as these bastards around here, but I recognized Connor's big belly just in time, so I didn't shoot."

"Ha ha, smart-ass," Connor remarked. Then he asked Jake, "Just tell me what the hell kinda party did you invite us to, and what the hell are you doing? Your man Steve told us some of it."

Jake answered, "I'll tell you all I can, but first, answer me why in the hell it took you so long to get here for Christ's sake?"

"Okay, listen," Connor started to explain, "I'm sorry. I'm mule-headed, but you pissed me off, calling me an asshole and telling me to shut up. So I was dragging my feet not believing you until Caleb straightened me out. He told me it all so I know I owe you a big apology."

"Listen, boys," Caleb interrupted, "you two can kiss and make up later. We've more important things to worry about right now. Jake, like Connor said, your man Steve told us some of what's going down, how about telling us the rest, but fast."

"So Steve's okay?" asked Jake.

"He is," Caleb said, "considering he is leaking from three or four bullet holes. They shot up Mason pretty bad too. EMTs will be here soon, Mae's called up half the state by now. Connor's got people north and south, stopping those other trucks."

Connor broke in, "So tell us already, what kind of shit we have left to clean up here."

Jake nodded and asked, "First, what do you boys have for ammo? I've got five rounds in this AR."

Caleb answered, "I have five clips and four rounds in my 06."

Connor added, "I have three rounds in the shotgun and two clips for my 9mm.

Jake stood up and said, "Let's do this. I'll take the 06. Connor, you take the AR. Maybe we can grab some more ammo from the guys around the corner. Caleb, you take the shotgun and a set of keys. Go back around to the theater. Cammie's in the little gym. Yell out though before going in. She's got a shotgun too. You two stay there until Connor and I get back to you."

"Here's the deal," Jake continued. "Raul is dead up front, along with a couple of his goons. His nephew and a couple others are dead by the side entrance, and there's three more down by Cammie."

"Man oh man, you've been a busy boy, Jake," Connor said. "You sure there's any left?"

Jake answered, "One truckload. It's by the loading docks. Rink was gonna use the school as a warehouse for Vortez's drugs. We'll keep them bottled up till help comes." No one got to say another word as three of Raul's men came running around the corner and opened fire.

Jake yelled to Caleb, "Go, Caleb, get to Cammie!" Caleb nodded and took off, Jake and Connor giving him cover as he ran to the door.

"Shit!" yelled Jake.

"Double shit!" Connor added as they both ducked back—bullets thudding into the trucks all around them.

"Damn it," Jake spat.

"What's wrong, Jake?" Connor asked.

Jake yelled, "I forgot to tell Caleb that Pastor Dean's in this up to his neck."

"Holy crap! Pastor Dean a drug dealer. What next, Mickey Mouse as their backup? Where's Dean now?" Connor asked.

"I think he's around the corner, so let's get these guys and nail his ass," Jake answered.

"One question, Jake, isn't this your work truck?"

"It is. So what?"

"Aren't those propane torch tanks sitting right above us?

"Oh shit! We've got to move. We'll run to the fountain. You go first. I'll cover you."

"Are you nuts? That's a hundred yards!" yelled Connor.

"Don't be such a wuss!" yelled Jake, grinning at Connor. Then Jake calmly stood up, firing Caleb's .30-06 off as fast as he could bolt it.

The gunman had been coming at them in a row, firing wildly; and for a man of Jake's skill, they were sitting ducks. Jake took the one on the left first, a head shot, killing him instantly. Then he shot the middle man twice in the chest, knocking him back and down for good. The last man wised up and dropped to the ground using his friend's body as a shield. Jake could see Connor was almost to the fountain, so he took off himself. He only made it about one hundred feet when the propane tanks blew, quickly followed by both trucks' gas tanks. Why it didn't blow sooner, Jake never could figure out. The blast knocked Jake to the ground, and he felt a searing pain in his back. Still able to get up, he hobbled to the fountain, taking cover behind it with Connor.

"You hit?" Connor asked.

"Something nailed me in the back," Jake answered. "How about you?"

"I took one in the leg. Hurts like a SOB," Connor said, showing Jake his leg.

Jake took a look at it, tearing off a piece of his shirt and wrapping it tightly around it, saying, "I don't think it will be fatal, but as ornery as you are, who knows!"

"Ha ha, very funny. Jesus, Jake, I can't believe you used to do this shit for a living!"

Jake looked at Connor. "What the hell you whining about? You've been sheriff for, what, twenty-eight years?"

"Thirty quiet years," replied Connor. "A few murders now and then, one bank robbery. Not this machine gun, things blowing up bullshit."

Jake asked, ducking down as another bullet thudded into the fountain, "So what you want to do, surrender?"

Sitting back up, Connor said, "The thought crossed my mind, but how about we just nail these bastards already so I can get back to my nice, quiet sheriff shit."

"Well, cuz," Jake said, taking a peek around the fountain from which they had a perfect view of the last semi and the loading docks, "it looks like Dean and about five or six guys left, and it seems they're going to make a break for it."

"Jake, what do you have left for ammo? I've got nine rounds."

"Same here," Connor said.

Jake held up his hand for "quiet" as he took aim at a guy sneaking up the passenger side of the truck. Connor watched as Jake waited, not a muscle moving. Suddenly, *boom*, Jake fired, nailing the guy just below the windpipe as he stepped on the running board to open the truck door. "Hell of a shot," Connor said to Jake as Jake ducked back down, taking fire from the last of the three men by the corner.

Jake turned to Connor. "Connor, that guy has to go! You draw his fire, and I'll nail his ass!"

Connor looked at Jake. "You're joking, right? What am I supposed to do? Jump up and wave my arms?

"You'll think of something," Jake replied with a smirk. Connor grabbed his Mag flashlight, put his hat on it, and raised it up in the air. It did the trick. The gunman opened up, blowing the hat and flashlight right out of Connor's hand. The gunman had raised himself up just enough to shoot, which was six inches too high. Jake's bullet caught him right between the eyes.

Connor stretched up and took a peek. "Messy, but nicely done," he said.

"Two coming up by the driver's side," Jake yelled as he fired, hitting the lead man and killing him. He shot the second one in the knee then finished him with the last round in his rifle. He put in the last clip and turned to Connor saying, "Four shots left."

"I've got three," Connor said, "so now what?"

"Now," Jake said, "now we pull a Custer and charge them because it looks like they're getting ready to use an RPG on us."

Connor yelled back, "This just gets better and better! You just said Custer and RPG, and we have seven damn bullets left between the two of us."

Jake just looked over at him with a grin and said, "So ya coming or what?"

Connor grinned back. "Oh hell! A Custer it is!" he shouted as he hobbled up, firing a shot at the man who came around the truck and pointed an RPG at them.

Connor and Jake were about four feet apart as they ran toward the truck and loading dock. Jake took out the RPG gunner, but not before he got his shot off. Connor would never forget the sound of that thing as it went between him and Jake, its hissing sounding like a thirty-foot rattlesnake. It hit the fountain, blowing it to hell and throwing Connor twenty feet ahead. He still had his gun in his hand as he landed, his senses going crazy. It was as if he was in a slow-motion TV scene. He could see Jake firing then dropping his rifle and reaching for one of the ARs lying by the three dead men on the corner. Connor could see a man by the truck, and he was pointing his rifle at Jake. So Connor, using both his hands to fire, shot his last two rounds at the man, not knowing if he hit him or not. As he blacked out, he said to himself, "It's all on you now, Jake, all on you."

Chapter 20

Once they had blown the loading dock gate open, Paco and Dean had the men load one truck as fast as they could. Then Paco said, "Maybe we should go leave the rest, just get away."

"No," yelled Dean, "I'm not leaving anything, and I'm not leaving without my brother. I want to see if Sarge killed O'Nell!"

"As you wish, partner," answered Paco, "but I'm taking this load out. If you get caught, just remember, you and your brother had better not talk. I know people who can get to you in any prison. And as for Sarge, you know he's dead. I'm afraid this Jake O'Nell was more macho than we counted on, much more."

Dean just shrugged his shoulders and said, "Maybe so, but I am going to find my brother and kill O'Nell myself!" Paco never answered; he just nodded as he, his driver, and two others took off.

Once they were in the truck, Paco looked in the mirror at Dean and said to the others in the truck, "If that preacher man lives, I'm gonna kill him first chance I get!" The others all nodded in agreement.

They drove around the school, running into Jake. As he fired at them, Paco's last thoughts were *O'Nell* and *How?*

Chapter 21

Dean said to the remaining men, "Let's finish this up. We load, find my brother, kill O'Nell, and leave here rich, okay, men?"

"Sounds like a plan," replied Sancho, who was the next man in charge of Raul's men.

Just as they started loading again, they heard gunfire coming from around the corner and again as the truck reached the front entrance. More shots were heard as the truck returned, ending with loud explosions in front of the school. Dean yelled, "What the hell? Sancho, send men around front and see what the hell is happening." Four men took off running toward the front of the school, only to run into Jake. Three men came back to the docks, one slightly wounded.

Sancho asked, "What happened?"

The wounded man answered, "We ran into someone around the side, and that son of a bitch can shoot."

"One man!" bellowed Dean. "One man, and they run from him, for Christ's sake!"

Sancho pointed his gun at the three men, saying, "The good pastor's right. You should have stayed and finished him. Now go back and kill him or die."

Now the three looked at one another, and the wounded man said, "Okay, Sancho, we'll do as you ask, but I think you will be joining us in hell shortly!" The three men turned and went around the corner, only to be met by Jake, and now Connor's gun fire—and then their own deaths.

Dean and Sancho looked at each other, now hearing not one but two guns firing. Dean said, "I think it's time to leave."

Dean watched as Connor and Jake made it to the fountain, and Jake started picking off Raul's men. Sancho tried to kill them with an RPG, only to die himself. Now Dean was scared and worried as he watched Connor shoot another man as Jake picked up a rifle and hid behind the corner. Dean knew he was trapped. Then he thought, as he looked at the blown gate, *or am I?* He thought, *Connor's down, so what if we go back in the school and lead Jake into a trap—we* meaning himself and the last two of Raul's men. Dean turned to the men and said, "Let's go back through the school. Grab a rocket in case we need to blow a gate. We'll grab a car up front and get the hell out of here." Dean took off running, heading through the gate back into the school, thinking as he ran, *Maybe there's a way out of this yet. If Jake follows us, we kill him. The girl has to be hidden somewhere here inside. We find her, kill her. I might be able to talk myself out of this yet.* The last two of Raul's men ran after Dean, grabbing the RPG as they did.

They had to use it on a gate about a hundred feet in. Then Dean said to them, "Now we hide and wait for O'Nell."

Chapter 22

Jake had been hit by a chunk of concrete from the fountain, striking him in the side of the head and back. The blow stunned him, slowing him down. When his rifle had run empty, his only thought was to get to one of the ARs lying by the three dead men at the corner.

Jake whirled around as he heard two quick shots behind him. He watched as a man fell by the semi, rifle in his hand. Looking to see Connor's head drop down, hands still holding the pistol he'd used to save Jake, Jake fired a burst at the loading dock. When no shots were fired back at him, he carefully went and checked the docks. Quiet had settled over the area.

Jake went and checked on Connor, relieved to find him alive but with a huge gash on the back of his head. Then Jake heard the explosion of an RPG come from the school. *Blowing a gate,* he thought to himself. He knew it was Dean and maybe some others. Jake took a minute to think and catch his breath. First, he put a rifle and two clips next to Connor, pointing it at the school. Then he thought, *No way am I going into the school through the gate.* He had another way, through the old part of the school, hoping Dean wouldn't think of it as he started out. His gaze fell down into the valley. Jake could see fires lighting the sky. "Damn," he said, "looks like there's been hell to pay in town. Hope everyone in Wineca is okay!"

Chapter 23

When Butch Harlowe arrived at the fire station, he was still having a hard time believing this was really happening, but he could tell by Connor's tone, he wasn't kidding. Butch loved his job and took it seriously, some thought too seriously at times, but he was good, and it was to pay off today. He wasted no time telling his deputies, posse members, and firefighters what he wanted. Larry, the fire chief, wasn't too happy to use their trucks for a roadblock, especially his pride and joy—a new 250-thousand-dollar ladder truck.

Butch was mentally trying to keep track of the time as they set up the roadblock. He also sent his deputy, Kyle, to borrow guns from a collector, Mr. Phia, or Mr. P for short, a block away. Butch then sent a couple of posse members over to the Sky View Apartments, ordering them to tell the residents to "get the hell out of those glass front apartments and shut all the lights off. Damn building is lit up like a big ol' Christmas tree for somebody to shoot at." He had another member go over to the clinic to have them call everybody in and to get ready for casualties.

Butch jumped up on top of his squad car and looked at the crowd, now numbering about forty or so. He yelled, "Listen up! This is the real deal. The sheriff said we got two semitrucks loaded with drugs and four to six bad-ass men each coming our way. He wants us to stop them if we can, use everything we've got. We're gonna try, but the sheriff doesn't want anybody taking crazy chances. We don't want any dead heroes."

Jeremy Henke, a school board member, spoke up, "So where's Connor at, and who says these trucks are coming?"

"The sheriff and Caleb Johnson are up at the school. They're helping Jake O'Nell. There's more of these guys up at the school. They killed Bob Haley, shot Mason Peevy, and an undercover man that works for Jake O'Nell, full of holes."

"I don't believe this," said Henke. "We're going on Jake O'Nell's word here?"

Hank Pond, another school board member, said, "I'm with Jeremy on this. We're gonna believe a drunken janitor on something like this? What you got to say, Butch?"

"God damn it!" Butch screamed. "We don't have time for you two assholes on this. Jake says Carl Rink is the leader in this whole damn deal, and I believe him. If Jake said dogs could talk and pigs flew, I'd believe him, and I'll tell you pompous asses why. First, Jake's no drunk. Second, he's the owner and CEO of SSBBKO, a company which has done one hell of a lot for this town and state. Lastly, Jake saved my cousin's life in Afghanistan. I believe what he says."

Pond said, "This is crazy. I've heard rumors about Jake having money, but CEO and owner of SSBBKO, that's a little hard to swallow."

Rich Mara, another school board member and Wineca's mayor, jumped in with "You two better believe it. I've known and worked with Jake all along, and remember, I've never trusted Rink. It was your vote, Mr. Pond, that got Rink hired. Are you in on this as well?" Hank looked around as people started to back away from him, staring at him with wondering eyes.

Hank yelled quickly, "Okay, okay, maybe I don't know about Jake for sure, but I only thought Rink was the most qualified, that's all! I don't know a thing about any of this."

Then Laney Moris, who was standing on top of the ladder truck, fired a shot from a gun that was almost as big as she was. You could hear a pin drop as she yelled, "Listen up, you jackasses, I'll tell you about Jake O'Nell. Two years ago when my dad was dying of cancer, Jake came to visit him every day until he was gone. He helped Mom and us girls through it, and after, he paid all our bills and paid off the mortgages on our house and store. When Mom asked him why, he told us how a long time ago, on a hot summer day, two little boys sat watching people eat ice cream at dad's store. It was Jake and Connor Hess. They couldn't afford to buy any, but my dad took them out two big cones and sent a bucket home with each of them for their families. The next day, Jake came in and told my dad that someday he would pay him back. When he handed Mom the receipts of the paid mortgages, he said, 'We're even now.' So that's who Jake O'Nell is, and if anybody else says a bad word about him again, I'll shoot them myself." She looked down directly at Mr. Henke and Mr. Pond and said, "You two point those guns in any direction but at those two trucks that's coming our way, I will shoot you!"

That's when one of Butch's deputies, Scot P., Mr. P's son, came up yelling, "Butch, Pearl just called! She's been listening to the scanner. Your trucks went by her place rolling like bats from hell. We've got a bunch of dad's guns here, along with what we have from the jail."

"Shit! Okay, people," Butch barked, "we got maybe five minutes. Anybody that don't have a gun and can halfway shoot, grab one and make damn sure to grab the right ammo. Anyone who can't shoot or doesn't have a gun, stay back. If somebody gets hit, you help get them to the clinic if ya can."

Larry yelled from the side street, "Terry can't get the plow started. He wants to know if he has time to jump it?"

"Hell no," yelled Butch, adding, "tell him to bring the brush truck or his own. I don't care, but I want that alley closed by the Panda Shop.

Butch looked around, mentally checking things off, happily noticing all the lights were off at the Sky View. Except one, right smack in the center of the building—old man Jarvis's condo, who else? Butch thought to himself, *You dumb, stubborn son of a bitch.*

As he turned back to the roadblock, he spotted Tyler Hewitt, rifle in hand, coming up the road. Following close behind was his twelve-year-old son, Travis, who was also toting a rifle. Butch ran over to him yelling, "What the hell you thinking, Tyler? Bringing your kid to this?"

"Listen, Butch, Travis can shoot better than you and me. My wife's at work, so no way was I leaving him home alone! So back off. You said you needed help, and we're here!" Tyler shouted back.

"Jesus!" Butch said, watching as eighty-year-old Mr. P. came toward them with what looked like his double-barrel elephant rifle. Alongside him came Reverend Standish from the Methodist Church, all six feet six of him, carrying a pistol. Butch threw up his hands and said, "The world's gone mad!"

Laney yelled, "Butch, they're here. They're at the top of the hill." Butch ran to the row of squad cars he'd had parked nose to nose as the first line of defense. Quiet settled in as Butch and the others watched and waited.

Nothing happened for a few minutes. Then the trucks came ahead slowly, stopping 250 feet away. Larry yelled, "What now, Butch?" Before Butch could even answer, guys started piling out of the trucks, opening fire as they did so with automatic rifles and one man getting ready to fire a RPG at them.

"Shit," Butch yelled, "shoot, SHOOT!" thinking he'd waited too long to open fire on them, but Laney had been ready. She nailed the RPG gunner just as he pulled the trigger, his body slamming back from Laney's 220 grain bullet from her .300 Magnum. The rocket veered to the left, plowing into Wineca's propane depot, which then proceeded to make the biggest fireworks show Wineca would ever see. Unfortunately, most of the people in the roadblock turned to watch, forgetting about what was coming down the road at them.

Red and three men were walking along beside the lead truck, using it as cover as it slowly came closer. Red had grabbed an RPG, readying it to fire. Butch, Laney, and Tatum Moris, who was one of Laney's younger sisters, had stayed focused. Butch took out one man, Laney another. Tatum took a shot at Red, hitting him in his left shoulder. Red was still able to fire the rocket, his aim dead on. Wineca's new ladder truck was blown into pieces, taking out half their barricade.

Laney was thrown fifty feet back into the wall of the bank. Butch was thrown sideways into a light pole by a second rocket, punching a hole in the line of squad cars. Butch could only sit there, unable to move, a surreal moment as things unfolded. Mr. P. came dashing out of nowhere, letting go with both barrels of that .458 caliber elephant gun, firing directly into the oncoming truck's engine, busting the block and stopping it dead, fifty feet from the barricade. The recoil from the gun knocked Mr. P. backward, and as he fell, his head smacked against the concrete, knocking him out cold. Butch could hear nothing, but his heart filled with pride as he watched the people of Wineca, his people—even with the pounding they'd taken in the last few minutes—hanging in, the wounded being pulled back to safety, and the fight still raging on. Nobody was going to run from this fight, that was a given.

Hank Pond took out the driver of the stalled truck as he jumped out firing. The last man walking with Red had knifed Jeremy Henke before Larry and Scott took him out, before they both got cut down by the big red-haired goon, as Butch thought of him. Scott dropped a couple of feet from his dad. Red shot Hank Pond in his left buttock as Hank dived for cover, which caused a lot of teasing for Hank for a lot of years.

Butch could see that if they didn't get the redhead soon, they were going to fail. Butch was starting to feel his hands again, so he tried to bring his pistol up, but it was a no go. Redhead saw him and started laughing as he came toward Butch. He was saying something to Butch, but Butch's ears were still ringing. He watched as Red brought his rifle up, figuring he was done. Butch sat stunned as Red's head exploded, stopping him in his tracks. He couldn't believe he was still alive and was amazed as he watched Travis Hewitt come over, give Red's body a kick, gun in hand and ready to fire again. Then he turned, giving Butch a big grin and a thumbs-up. Butch grinned back before he blacked out. His last thought was, *Maybe bringing a kid to a gunfight wasn't such a bad thing after all.*

Tatum Moris, who was the assistant fire chief, had been on the far side of things next to the Panda Shop. She'd done her share of firing, not knowing if she'd hit anyone or not, but had been pouring lead into the tires making sure they stayed put. Now as the firing stopped, she could see that all the men in the first truck were down and out for good, but it had cost them big. It looked to her that of the thirty or so that had manned the barricades, only a handful could still function, and she couldn't see her big sister Laney anywhere.

Tatum's big problem now was lack of ammo for her rifle. She wondered how anyone else was on that end. Then she realized that Butch hadn't moved since Travis had shot the big red-headed bastard. She knew Larry was dead simply by the way he was lying so, basically, people were kind of standing around dazed, a few helping with the wounded. Tatum decided that somebody had to take charge, so she did—and big time. She spotted Kyle, one of his arms dangling as he checked on Butch. She yelled to Kyle, "Get yourself to the clinic and get us some more help up here. We need to get these wounded back and taken care of." As Kyle took off she added, "You see anybody with a gun, send them to me. Ask for ammo, any kind ya can get, and get it up here to us."

The guys in the second truck had backed off when Red went down, which was a lucky break for the blockaders. Had they kept coming, they might have made it through. Tatum was keeping an eye on them as she dialed the sheriff's office and waited for Mae to answer, and she answered on the first ring. Tatum spoke right up, "Mae, they hammered us good out here. Butch and Larry are down. We stopped one truck, but there's another load of these bastards out there yet. If any help's coming, have them set up at the stoplights. We got fires burning and no way to put them out."

"I know about the fires," Mae replied. "We're on fire here ourselves. Help's on the way. The Jonesville boys will be there soon, and more units are coming, including SWAT."

Tatum had turned to look at the sheriff's office and jail, which had caught on fire from the propane explosion. "Okay, Mae, you've done enough. Now get the hell out of there!" Only silence came. "Shit" was all Tatum got to say as she watched two men get out of the second truck with RPGs. Tatum yelled, "Incoming!" as she hit the ground. One rocket took out another fire truck, and the second hit Sky View Apartments. Tatum figured that was coming, just too hard for the smart-asses to resist, that one apartment shining like a big bull's-eye. She sat up and picked up her rifle, emptying the last three rounds in it at the gunners, making them dive for cover.

Mr. P., now sitting back up, yelled, "Somebody take my .458. I've got six shots left, but I busted my shoulder." Tinker Rand, a Wineca fireman, piped up and yelled, "I'll take it. My pistol's empty."

Tatum yelled out, "Anybody with ammo come with me! We have to get those guys before they blow up the whole damn town." She was looking to see where she could pick up a gun when she saw, of all things, her two youngest sisters, Aubree and Addy, running toward her, one carrying a large bag and the other her mom's 7mm Magnum deer rifle. As they approached her, Tatum asked in a stern voice, "What the hell are you doing here?"

Aubree answered, "Mom was coming up to help, and we were bringing ammo, but we found Laney by the bank hurt bad! Mom and Avery are taking her to the clinic." Addy handed Tatum their mom's gun and said, "Mom said to tell you to get these guys already so we can clean things up around here. Oh, and she says she loves you."

"We love you too," Aubree said, "but we need to get going now. We gotta go get some of these guys fixed up." Both girls took off on a dead run, leaving Tatum shaking her head as she loaded her mom's rifle.

Tinker said, "I'll be damned, those are quite the sisters you got there."

Tatum looked at him and said, "Tink, don't get any ideas. They're both under eighteen, and I am holding a loaded rifle! Now here's the plan. We use the cars parked on the left as cover and the retaining wall. Let's go!" Tinker and his brother Roy took off first, with Tinker yelling, "Just like football, Roy, you and me open the hole!"

"You got it!" Roy shouted back as they reached the two cars parked along the street, about a hundred yards from the semi. Roy's first shot took out a gunner, and Tinker stood up calmly, firing four rounds into the engine, steam and smoke bellowing out. Tatum and three others came up by Tinker and Roy, firing on the truck, but the second RPG gunner was still able to fire, hitting his target and blowing the two cars sky-high. Tatum was blown back fifteen feet. As she blacked out, her last thought was *That's weird, it sounds like the*

Dukes of Hazzard are coming. What she was hearing was a Dixie horn sounding "Charge," and it was from Billy Zale's truck. The Jonesville boys had arrived.

Jonesville was a little town about six miles from Wineca. The people there claimed their town was founded by some kin of John Paul Jones, and they prided themselves in being fighting sons of bitches like he was. Billy Zale's truck was in the lead. It was a big jacked-up mud bogger, Billy's pride and joy. It had chrome rims, custom paint, and a roll bar with stadium lights along it. A hundred yards from the semi, he pulled up and lit that rig up like a Christmas tree, which gave the Jonesville boys in the other trucks one hell of a target. They all piled out firing, and the gunner's attention was also turned to Billy's truck. As the gunner pointed the RPG at Billy's truck, Billy's brother, an Iraq war veteran who was riding shotgun in Billy's truck, yelled, "Incoming, everybody get the hell out!" Everybody bailed—everybody but Billy, that is. Billy's truck had everything except a working inside door handle. He'd put off getting it fixed, saying it was "No big deal to roll down the window and open it from the outside." Except for today. Billy had just started to open his door when the rocket hit, sending Billy and his truck to heaven.

For all the years to come, anytime a round is bought at the one and only bar in Jonesville, the toast is to Billy and his truck, with the ad lib of "If only it hadn't been for that damn handle!"

Billy's death motivated the rest of the Jonesville boys, which included Billy's two brothers, to seek some payback on the last of Raul's men. Fifteen rifles poured it to them, killing the three men left in less than five minutes. Wineca's War on Drugs, as it was called by the press in the days to come, was over.

Nine thugs killed and thirty-five million in drugs seized by the authorities, leaving the town with six dead, thirty-eight wounded, and half the town burned or blown up. You might think of it as a hollow victory, but not so. The people of Wineca and Jonesville, they figured outgunned and with almost no time to prepare, they'd still kicked ass and were damn proud of it!

Chapter 24

Jake took one last look down at the town and thought, *No matter what or how long it takes, Rink and Dean are going to pay for this!* As he went through a small side door into the old original part of the school, Jake crept cautiously up the hall. The kids called this hall the "hall of doom." They named it to psych out opposing teams that had to go through it to get to the locker rooms. The walls of the hall were covered with hundreds of pictures of Wineca students, athletes, coaches, and teachers from over the last fifty years. This was Jake's favorite part of the school and was why he made sure it was preserved and untouched when they built the new school.

Jake paused at his favorite spot in the hall, the place where his family's pictures hung, including one from the year before the accident when Jake was named coach of the year. His entire family was in it. He remembered thinking at the time, *Boy, it doesn't get any better than this!* and how he was a lucky man!

As Jake looked at the picture, he said, "Hey, gang, thanks for looking out for me today." He added, "Korrine, honey, this Cammie seems like a real sweetie. I think you'd like her, but I guess you know that already, don't you." "Love you guys," he whispered and blew them a kiss. As he started to step away, he turned back saying, "Bridget, baby, sleep tight, don't let the bed bugs bite." Jake took a deep breath and wiped the tears from his eyes before turning back to the darkness. As he took off down the hall, he swore he heard Korrine saying to him, as she always did before a big game or a hunt, "Go get 'em, tiger! Grrrr!"

Jake reached the door to the gym, pausing to listen before slowly opening it. He was in time to see four shapes heading toward the theater. As they went past the light of an exit sign, Jake swore as he spotted Dean holding a gun on Cammie and pushing her along with two of Raul's men following close behind. *Where's Caleb?* he wondered.

Jake watched until he lost sight of them as they entered the theater. He crossed the gym, being still wary of an ambush. He was taking no chances and decided to go around to the front of the theater to use a different door than Dean's bunch had used.

As he opened the door, he was just in time to see Raul's two men go charging out the exit door, guns firing. Dean flew out the door right behind them, dragging Cammie with him. Dean began shouting, "Don't shoot him, you idiots! We can use the sheriff as a hostage!"

"Don't move, Sheriff, or you're dead where you stand!"

Jake thought, *Damn it, Connor, what in hell are you doing?* He wasted no time as he went to the controls to the big overhead door to the outdoor theater. He was determined not to let these guys get Cammie, and now Connor too, into a vehicle to escape. He hit the up button and dropped flat on the floor, rifle ready to fire. Being only partially hidden, he knew it was a gamble, but loss of blood and fatigue was starting to get to him, plus he was on edge.

The two gunmen spun around, rifles ready, but Jake gave them no chance, firing as fast as he could pull the trigger, and the bullets hitting their marks. Both men, riddled with bullets, dropped and were dead when they hit the ground. Jake rolled out the door searching for and spotting Dean. He was backed up against the wall using Cammie as a shield and a pistol jammed in her side.

Dean yelled, "Jake, don't move! And drop that gun, or I pull this trigger, and that goes for you too, Sheriff." Jake looked over in surprise. He was not seeing Connor standing twenty feet from him as he expected, but Sheriff Leo Cullen of Rockbridge County, the little county that bordered Crawfish County to the east.

Jake stood up, saying, "Howdy, Leo."

Leo nodded and answered, "Hello, Jake. Thanks for taking out those scum suckers! They just gunned down Davey and had me dead to rights."

Jake could see Davey's body lying by the steps. "Shit, Leo, Davey was a good kid. I'm sorry."

"Thanks, Jake. He was the best, a real good kid." Pausing a moment, Leo asked, "Now how do you want to handle this?"

Jake didn't answer right away. Instead, he looked at Cammie and asked, "Cammie, did Caleb find you?"

"He found me okay," she yelled, "but I never got a chance to warn him about this asshole holding me! Dean just shot him with no warning!"

Dean rapped Cammie on the head and yelled, "What is wrong with you three morons? I have a gun on this bitch, and you carry on like you were at a tea party. I'm in charge here, don't you see that?"

"All I see," Jake remarked, "is a preacher that is lower than any snake and is too stupid to know it and that he's done for!" Jake turned and looked at Leo and asked, "That the way you see it, Leo?"

"About right, Jake," Leo replied with a grin, then went on saying, "Mr. Preacher Man, you drop that gun, you live. If you hurt that girl, die here and now!"

"Listen, you two assholes," Dean started to say, but just then, the school rocked from an explosion on the far side.

After the noise died down, Jake started laughing, long and hard. Looking at his puzzled audience, Jake turned to Leo and asked, "Want to hear a funny story?"

"Sure," Leo replied with a smirk on his face, "I like a good laugh, and, ah, does it have anything to do with the big bang we just heard?"

Smiling, Jake said, "Oh, it does! You see, I think we just heard Pastor Dean's ugly brother, Mr. Carl Rink, taking himself a one-way trip to hell. I bet Rink tried to sneak back into the school using my back door, but what he didn't know was that Sarge rigged it with a booby trap."

"Now that is funny," Leo said with a chuckle. "Nothing like going out with a bang."

Dean yelled, "You sons of bitches!" He shot Cammie in the side as he did. As Cammie fell to the ground, Dean's gun turned on Jake. Both Jake and Leo fired at the same time, Jake's bullet taking Dean's right ear off, grazing his skull. Leo's bullet busted Dean's shoulder, knocking Dean down and the gun out of his hand. Jake bent down and picked the gun up, then grabbed Dean by the hair and pulled him about twenty feet from Cammie.

"Leo, please watch this pile of garbage for me," Jake said. "I have to see to Cammie."

"My pleasure," Leo replied as he walked over to Dean.

Just then, Connor came hobbling around the corner and stumbled up the stairs across the stage. He slid down the wall just a few feet from Jake and Cammie, saying, "Sorry, Jake, looks like I'm late again. How is she?"

Jake said, "Not good, but she won't let me touch her until I check on Caleb."

"Connor," Cammie said, "tell him to go. Caleb was shot, and I have to talk to you. Please!"

Connor looked up at Jake. "All right, I'll go," Jake said, shaking his head. "Connor, talk some sense into her while I'm gone." He took off at a run across the theater.

"Sorry, Leo, that I didn't say hello right away. So how's things going in your county?" Connor asked with a big grin as he slid closer to Cammie. Cammie whispered into Connor's ear. Leo didn't answer, just shook his head while holding his pistol on Dean's whining head.

Jake found Caleb, still alive, along the wall by Sarge's body. Jake asked, "How bad ya hit?"

"Bad enough," Caleb whispered. "It's close to my lung, I think. I was hurting like hell, but I found some shit on this soldier boy here. I think it was morphine 'cause I can't feel hardly anything right now. But you need to listen to me, Jake! That fricking Pastor Dean, he's the one who shot me, and he has Cammie. I didn't have a chance."

"I know," Jake said. "It's my fault. I never told you about Dean. We have Dean, but he shot Cammie. I don't know how bad yet. She insisted that I check on you first."

"That figures," Caleb said. "She's quite the gal. The real deal, Jake, so don't you lose her. You go fix her up. I'll be okay until help comes. Oh, and by the way, you done good here today, Jake. I'm damn proud of you."

"Back at you," Jake said with a smile. "You're not too bad for being a worn-out fossil, that is."

Caleb chuckled and said, "Just go, you smart-ass. Get somebody here before my buzz wears off."

Jake went back to the theater, telling Cammie and the others that Caleb was hanging in there. He finally rolled Cammie over to look at her wound. He didn't like the looks of it, but there was little he could do. He plugged the hole with more of his tattered shirt and wrapped his belt around Cammie, pulling it tight to at least help stop the blood loss.

Chapter 25

Hearing a noise, Jake looked up to see a man coming around the corner with a rifle. Jake grabbed for his gun, Leo and Connor doing the same. The man yelled, "Whoa, whoa, guys! It's me, Johnny Dodd." He was one of Leo's deputies.

"Jesus!" Leo yelled. "You damn near got your ass shot off." Then, seeing the shape the young man was in, Leo said, "HOLY SHIT, Johnny, what in hell happened to you?"

Johnny's uniform was torn to pieces, his hair singed, there was a gash on his cheek, and he was walking with a limp. Johnny answered, "You sent us to help Harlan and his men. We done good at first. We blew out all their tires, but those damn bastards wouldn't stop, and they were armed to the teeth. Harlan and two of his troopers bought it taking care of the first truck. We shot that second truck to pieces. Derek and Charlie got hit, and then it got by us. Rita was pissed! She said no way they're getting away." Johnny started to choke up.

Leo said, "Go on, Johnny, tell us what happened."

Johnny took a breath and continued, "She took her squad car and rammed them head-on. Her squad and the truck both blew up. We lost her, Sheriff."

Sheriff Cullen looked right at Johnny and said, "You stand tall now, you hear. We lost Davey too. He's laying over there on those steps about twenty feet from you. Okay, now you listen. You done your job, and Rita and Davey did theirs."

Johnny looked at the sheriff and said, "You can count on me, sir. I'll be all right."

Jake turned to Johnny and asked, "What's the word from Wineca?"

"It's bad, Jake, real bad. They stopped both trucks, but it cost big. Half the town is on fire, and a hell of a lot of people down."

"Shit! We got any help coming?" Jake asked.

"I brought two EMT squads from Rim-Rock with me," Johnny said. "They're taking care of Mason and that other fella at the entrance. MedFlights and more squads are coming in from all over. Maybe we could get one for the lady."

"That's good," Jake said. "We have a man down inside too, and he's hurt pretty bad."

"Well, Leo," Jake said, "that leaves only one thing to finish here, and I hope you don't try to stop me, because no way is Dean Chadfee going to trial and weasel his way out of this with some kind of a plea deal. This whole thing is on him. Too many good people died today, and I'm sorry, but he has to pay for his sins and right now."

Leo answered, "No problem, Jake. Rita and Davey were family, so you or me, it doesn't matter." Leo asked Johnny, "That okay with you?"

Johnny looked at Jake and his sheriff, knowing he would go to hell and back for men like them. He nodded okay and said, "I just can't believe how that dumb pastor grabbed for that gun, shot up like he was. Stupid, just plain stupid." He finished with a grin.

Dean had been listening, planning what his next moves would be, when what they were saying finally sunk in. He yelled, "You shit heads! You can't just kill me. I have rights. It's bad enough I'm sitting here bleeding to death. You have to read me my rights and take me in."

Leo put his gun to Dean's head, and Jake did the same. Leo said, "Dean Chadfee, you have the right to remain silent! Goodbye, asshole!"

As their fingers tightened, Connor yelled, "Jake, Leo, wait!"

Jake spun around, yelling at Connor, "Christ, Connor, you can't feel sorry for this piece of shit!"

"Hell no, Jake, I'm with you guys. It's Cammie. She has to talk to you and Leo. Please listen to her. It's important."

"All right," Jake said, pulling his gun back. Leo did the same and turned to Johnny, telling him, "Watch the good pastor for us. If his nose twitches, put a bullet between his eyes."

"You got it, Sheriff," Johnny answered as he pointed his gun at Dean with obvious glee.

Leo and Jake went over to Cammie. Jake knelt down. "What is it, Cammie? How can you feel sorry for this asshole for Christ's sake? He shot Caleb and you!"

"Listen to me, Jake," Cammie pleaded. "I know all he's done. I agree he should pay, but it's because I might not live that I need him. I kept one secret from you, Jake. I have a nine-year-old son, and his name is Nicki. He's a great young man. Do you understand, Jake?"

Jake nodded and spoke lightly to Cammie, "You don't want anyone to know his father's dead, but what's that got to do with Dean?"

"I want him to marry us, Jake, if you will have me. I know I'm hurt bad. If I die, I want my son to have a father—a great father like you. If I make it, we can get a divorce. I'll not take a penny of your money. I swear it in front of these two noble officers of the law."

Jake was stunned. He stammered, "You're lying here shot, and you want to get married to me?"

Connor piped up, "You'll have to forgive him, ma'am, sometimes he's a little slow."

"Thanks, Connor, you're such a big help," Jake said before he continued. "I'll do it. So that's why you won't let us shoot Dean, because you want us to get married, and he needs to do the ceremony?"

"Yes, exactly. Sheriff Leo can give me away, if he will, since I have no parents to do it. Connor can be your best man, and Johnny can be our witness." She looked around at Leo, Connor, and Johnny. "I want all three of you to be godfathers to Nicki, if you will. Promise to help Jake if I don't make it."

Leo looked down at Cammie and said, "I'd be honored to give you away and be a godfather."

Johnny chimed in, "I'm in."

Connor sat up as straight as he could then answered, "You can count on me. I'll make sure these 'Jack-o'-Napes' don't corrupt your son!" They all chuckled.

"Okay then," Jake said, "let's do this. Leo, drag that asshole over here on the double so we can get Caleb and Cammie to the hospital."

Leo went over and grabbed Dean by the hair, telling him as he pulled him to his feet, "Today is your lucky day, scumbag. You don't get to die."

Dean stood there and said, "Yeah, I heard, and my answer is, fuck you! I'm bleeding to death here, my life ruined, and that slut wants me to marry them so she can die happy for her son. Oh boohoo! Fuck you!"

Jake didn't say a word. He got up, walked over, and started slapping Dean's head back and forth, telling him, "You call her a slut again, you die!" Dean nodded. He could see in Jake's eyes that he had crossed the line, and he was as close to death as he'd ever been in his whole life. Jake went on, "Listen, you piece of shit. I'll make you the only deal you're going to get. No way are you just walking away from this, so here's my offer. Marry us now, you go to this island near St. John's I own, and you spend the rest of your life there. You'll have food, books, hell, even women, but no phones and no electronics. We'll have Johnny here take you to Lakewood, get ya all fixed up. But you will talk to no one at any time."

Jake turned around. "Leo, Connor, will that work for you?"

Connor spoke up first, "If that's the way you want it, we'll back you all the way."

Leo glanced at Connor then looked at Jake. "Your call, Jake, but no way Johnny does this alone! He'll need help."

Johnny jumped in, "I can get him to Lakewood, and I'll call my cousin. He's an EMT, and my brother-in-law-to-be is a posse man for Cambridge. I'll get him to help too."

"That'll work," Jake said, "but until either Leo, Connor, or I get a hold of you, Dean talks to no one, and one of you stays with him at all times, even in the can. He is not to be alone for even one second, you got it?" Johnny nodded. "I'll pay you fifty thousand dollars each for the job."

"No shit!" Johnny cheered.

"No shit," answered Jake.

Connor added, "If he talks to anybody, Johnny, at any time, you bring him back to Leo and me. He'll either disappear, or we'll cut him loose and tell the world how he helped us nail Raul Vortez."

Connor turned to Jake and asked, "Um, we did nail him, didn't we, Jake?"

"Yeah, we got him," Jake said with a laugh. "Right now he is having a long talk with Satan. But enough talk. Let's get on with this."

Dean looked at Jake and said through clenched teeth, "All right, I'll agree to this, but you had better not screw me on this."

"Listen, Chadfee, when I make a deal, I keep it. Now get on with it. Johnny, as soon as we're done, he's all yours, and you can get him out of here."

Johnny pulled Dean back to his feet and pushed him over by Jake and Cammie. Leo leaned over and said, "Pastor, the short and sweet version please."

Pastor Dean started the service by asking, "Who gives this woman to be wed today?"

"I do," answered Leo.

"Now," Dean continued, "repeat after me with your full names please. Cammila, you first."

"My name is Cammila Marie Martinez."

"Mine is Jacob Hercules O'Nell."

"No shit!" Connor yelped as he busted out laughing. "I finally know what the *H* stands for—Hercules."

"Oh, and like Beauregard is any better," Jake barked.

"Jesus," Dean yelled. "Will you two shut the hell up already!" After completing the vows, Dean said, "Now all we need are the rings."

Connor handed Jake his and said, "Use mine. Hazel would like that."

Johnny stepped forward, saying, "I have my girlfriend's engagement ring in my pocket. Will you use that, Ms. Cammie?"

"I'd be honored," she replied with a smile. "Jake and I'll get you a new one."

After the exchange of the rings, Dean said, "You may now kiss the bride." Jake leaned over and gave Cammie a long kiss while hoots and clapping came from the three lawmen.

Leo thought to himself, *This has got to be the goddamnedest wedding in history. The bride shot, the groom and best man shot, bruised, and blood dripping from them, four guns pointed at the pastor during the entire ceremony, all while fires burned, and it isn't over yet.*

Jake turned and hauled off and punched Pastor Dean in the jaw, knocking him down, yelling, "That was for old Bob and Caleb." Jake pulled the pastor up to his feet and belted him again, adding, "That's for Cammie."

Johnny jumped in before Jake could hit Dean again. "That's enough, Mr. O'Nell. He has to be able to walk to my car, remember?"

"Get him out of here, Johnny, and you make sure he draws up those wedding papers as soon as he can."

"Got it," Johnny replied as he pulled a dazed Dean up, putting the handcuffs on him. Johnny stopped and turned around. "Hey, fellas, one more thing before I go. You think your middle names stink? My mom wanted a girl something bad, so they named me Johnny Joyful Kelly."

Leo, Connor, Cammie, and Jake all looked at each other. Cammie started to giggle first, and then they all busted out laughing.

Jake slid down between Cammie and Connor and said, "That's about it for me, folks," and he promptly passed out. Leo looked at the ground where Jake had walked and stood, only now noticing all the blood on the cement. "Christ," said Leo, "Jake's leaking all over the place. I didn't even know he'd been hit."

"It figures," Connor said. "Jake here's one tough SOB." As he went on, he began to slur, "I really screwed up with Jake here, Leo, and he owns an island." That was the last word Connor said as he passed out too.

Leo said to himself, "That figures, they leave it all up to the old fat guy to finish cleaning the mess up." Leo took out his radio, hoping to call in some help or find out anything from anybody. Leo called into the radio, "This is Sheriff Leo Cullen from Rockbridge County. I'm assisting on a scene at Wineca High School. I need help. We have officers down. I repeat, officers down!"

Mae's voice came on the radio, "Sherriff, it's me, Mae. I'm calling from our mobile command center. We lost our office in the fight."

"No shit? The whole office?" Leo asked.

"No shit," answered Mae, "and we got all you need coming your way."

Just then, a bullet hit the wall just above Leo's head, and another hit him in the leg. He took cover behind Cammie's little smart car, wishing it was a hell of a lot bigger than it was. As he ducked down, he yelled into the radio, "I'm taking fire! I could use a SWAT team right about now or anybody with a goddamn gun!"

Chapter 26

When Paco's truck had wrecked coming back into the parking lot, the two men in the back had jumped out and ran into the woods on the south side. They were hoping to find the highway and hijack a car and get away, but they were city-born and raised and got lost. They finally had to go back to the burning truck, their only beacon to get them back to the school. They'd waited for a chance when the big sheriff was alone, and he was the only thing keeping them from finding a car to steal in the school's parking lot. They'd taken cover behind the semi's trailer, and that was mostly burned out by then. Luckily for Leo, they only had handguns and couldn't shoot worth shit!

"Sheriff Cullen" came a new voice on Leo's radio. This is Sergeant DJ Dunn of Ameryville SWAT Team. We're at the front of the school now. What's the plan?"

Leo yelled into the radio, "I'll fire four quick shots. When them assholes shoot back, you find 'em and take 'em out!" Leo didn't wait for an answer, firing four shots toward the burning truck. The two guys started firing wildly back.

DJ came back on the radio, "We got them spotted, Sheriff. They're down low behind that smoldering big rig. With the smoke and cover, it's going to be a bitch to get them quick."

"Well, son," Leo answered, "it's gonna have to be quick. We have people dying here. How much help you got?"

"There's six on my team, and last I heard, there's like two hundred units coming, EMTs, firetrucks, and police. Hell, we passed twenty-five units to get here first."

"What?" Leo asked DJ. "You don't like to be late when someone invites you to a party?"

"You got it. Who doesn't want first chance at the cake?" DJ answered. "Sheriff, I'm going to have half my team try to flank them."

"No time," Leo replied. "If I get these guys to show themselves, can you take them?"

"You bet. My snipers will get 'em, but how you gonna get—" was all DJ got to say. DJ and his team watched Leo toss out his gun, pull out a big hunting knife, and yell, "Come on, you chicken-shit bastards, I'm out of bullets, so I'll just have to show you what an old fat sheriff can do with just a little ol' hunting knife!" Leo started walking toward the truck.

The two men did just what he had hoped, coming out and away from the truck. One started saying, "Now you die, Mr. Fat—" That was all he was able to say before the SWAT team riddled them with bullets, firing until both men went down.

Leo called on the radio again, asking Mae, "Mae, you still there?"

"I'm here," she answered. "What happened?"

"Just a couple problems came up," Leo answered. "But we're good now. Any chance we could get a MedFlight or two up here or some rescue squads?"

"You'll have a dozen units there in under five minutes. About half the state is coming, and the rest is on hold. There's at least five more coming from Iowa. They should be here in less than fifteen minutes. Oh, and the governor called. He said if you need anything, just ask, and he will get it to us."

"No shit?" Leo said with a laugh. "Maybe I should have voted for the guy. One more thing, Mae, you'd better get a bomb squad up here too. We've had one explosion already, and there may be more IEDs hidden throughout the school. Good work, Mae."

Chapter 27

DJ and his team came over to Leo after they had checked out the two men and verified they were both down for good. DJ stuck his hand out. "Sheriff, I'm DJ Dunn, and this is my team. You're Lead on this. What do you want us to do?"

"Well, first of all, do you have a doctor on your team?" Leo asked.

"No doctor, but we all have EMT training, and Corporal Scully here was a combat medic for the Marines."

"Okay, Corporal." Leo pointed to the outdoor stage area. "You go look at our three wounded over there on the stage. DJ, you and the rest of your team go into the school. We have another man down in there." Leo gave DJ the directions to the location where Caleb was. "Go very carefully. I don't know what's in there. Just get him, bring him back out here, and work on him out here. When the bomb squad gets here, they can sweep the school for bombs and any lingering bad asses."

DJ nodded, motioned to his team, and took off. When they got closer to the school, DJ said to his team, "Looks like the sheriff was right about an explosion." They could smell the smoke, and the sprinklers were going.

Chapter 28

That explosion was exactly as Jake had guessed. It was Carl Rink who got caught in Sarge's booby trap. He'd gotten tired of waiting for anyone else to come out the front, and no way was he going to go the way Jake had, not after Jake damn near shot him. It had come to him that maybe Jake's truck was in that little picnic area that he had caught a few kids skipping out to now and then.

Carl was feeling pretty smug when he turned the corner, and yes indeed, there was Jake's truck. His joy was short-lived as he looked to find no keys in the ignition, nor above the driver's sun visor, in the ashtray, or glove box. He was even more pissed at Jake, saying to himself, "Why didn't Jake leave the keys in the truck? Who the hell would steal a piece of crap like this?" *Okay,* Rink thought to himself, *I'll go back to the school. Dean will look for me there anyways. I'll use Jake's own entrance that that guy Steve had found.* He grabbed a three-foot piece of pipe from Jake's truck, swinging it back and forth, dreaming how good it would feel to bash Jake's head in with it. His brother would be so proud of him, and then the best part was he would have that Martinez woman all to himself. Payback time for what happened to him in Vegas.

After that, he would use his share of the money to go to a country with young girls and no rules.

Those were the last perverted thoughts going through his head as he pulled open the door, not hearing the beep. The bomb blew Rink and his perverted thoughts to hell in a couple of hundred pieces, Rink's head flying up and back, crashing through the windshield on Jake's truck and landing on the seat. The truck keys fell out of the passenger-side sun visor, landing next to Rink's head—with that bit of God's irony only known to Rink's sightless eyes.

Afterward, when all was said and done, Jake's truck was scrapped. No one wanted it with Rink's blood in it, and for many years after the battle, if little kids found anything that looked like a bone, the big kids would scare them by saying it was a bone from Principal Rink, and he would come looking for his bones!

Chapter 29

Corporal Scully checked on Connor first; as she was checking him out, Connor came to. Seeing this good-looking redhead kneeling beside him, he said, "Well, I'll be damned. There is a heaven, with redheaded angels."

Scully smiled. "Thanks, but you ain't dead, and I'm no angel. I'm Corporal Scully with the Ameryville SWAT. Good to meet you."

"Glad to meet you. I'm Sheriff Connor Hess. Think I'll make it?"

"You will," she answered. "Leg wound's mostly stopped bleeding. Gash on the head, nothing that eight to ten stitches shouldn't fix, and maybe a concussion, no doubt."

"Now to your friend here," she said, rolling Jake over. "Holy shit, Sheriff, do you know who this is?" Without waiting for Connor to reply, she went on, "Captain Jake O'Nell!"

"Yep," Connor said, "that's Jake O'Nell, all right. He's my cousin, and that's his wife next to him. Do you know him?"

"Jesus, Sheriff, if you were a marine in Afghanistan, you'd know this cousin of yours. He saved a lot of our guys and sent a hell of a lot of Taliban to their virgins. These guys around here must have had no idea who in hell's school they were messing with!" Scully had been working on Jake the whole time she talked.

Connor answered, "No, Ms. Scully, they didn't. For some reason, they assumed that all they had to deal with was an old man and a part-time drunk janitor."

"Well," Scully said, "the captain's got a couple wounds in the back, lots of cuts and loss of blood. He'll make it. Now let's look at Mrs. O'Nell." When she did, Scully muffled "crap" to herself and immediately called on the radio, "I need an ETA on a med-chopper. We need it now!"

A response came over the radio that the chopper would be landing in three minutes. DJ and his men came out of the school carrying Caleb just as the chopper landed. They put Cammie and Caleb on the chopper and Jake on the first ambulance to arrive. As they waited for more backup units to arrive, DJ turned to Scully and said, "That was Jake O'Nell's godfather. He told us Jake was a marine, and he took out these guys that we're finding everywhere. Is this the Jake O'Nell you told us about?"

"It sure is," she answered. "I told you guys he was hell on wheels, nothing but the real deal."

"That he is," replied DJ.

Connor spoke up, saying, "I hate to interrupt you when you're talking about Jake here, but just for the record, I took out a couple bad guys myself, and do I have a ride coming for me? This leg is bleeding again."

Scully ran over to Connor. "Sorry, Sheriff, I didn't mean to forget you. Your ride's about five minutes out."

Connor smiled and said, "Ill forgive you on two conditions. First, tell me your full name, and if you're available, will you go on a date with me? I really do think you look like an angel."

Scully never knew for sure why she said what she did, but she answered, "Okay, I'll go out with you, and my name is Mattilda Scully, but everyone calls me Matti."

DJ yelled into his radio, "Guess what, guys, Matti's real name is Mattilda. I told you!"

Scully yelled into her radio, "Listen up, assholes, the first one of you that calls me anything but Matti or Corporal Scully, I'll shoot, got it!"

The ambulance arrived for Connor, who demanded that Scully ride with him. The unit was from Kellsville, 150 miles from Wineca. Connor was amazed how people from Wisconsin and Iowa—hell, the whole United States of America—were willing to help each other in times like these. Connor was on the verge of passing out when he said, "Be there when I wake up, Matti." He heard her say "I will" just as he blacked out.

Chapter 30

All this time, Sheriff Cullen had been organizing the sweep of the school, getting the fire trucks and men to put out the fires, arranging things so Davey's and Bob Haley's bodies were kept separate from the drug dealers, and meeting with SWAT members to keep things organized. Then a SWAT team leader noticed Leo's blood-soaked pant leg and the pool of blood by his shoe. He said, "Sheriff, we got this. Maybe you should head to the hospital and get yourself checked out."

Leo looked down. "Damn, I forgot all about that. Might explain why I'm getting woozy." He was the last casualty in Crawfish County's drug war.

After Leo was taken to the hospital, DJ, his team, and a couple more SWAT teams were taking a well-earned break. DJ turned to one of the SWAT team men, whom he knew was a former Navy Seal, and asked, "Is this what it's like over there, bombs going off, fires, and bodies everywhere?"

The former Navy Seal answered, "No, it's nothing like this, it's worse, much worse." He went on, "I'd heard of this O'Nell"—he looked at the bodies—"I thought it was mostly just marine bullshit talk, but with twenty-three down, God, I'm glad he was on our side. These guys must have been nuts to try this at Jake O'Nell's school!"

"Word is," DJ said, "they assumed all they would be dealing with was an ornery old man and a drunken part-time custodian."

"Bad intel," the Seal said. "It'll get ya every time."

"Yeah," chuckled DJ as he looked at the row of bodies, "really bad intel!"

Epilogue

Eight Months Later

Leo limped into the side meeting room of the church and asked Jake, as they shook hands, how it felt to be the new sheriff of Crawfish County. Jake answered, "Too soon to tell. How's the retirement suiting you?"

"Not bad at all," Leo replied.

"Well, Leo, I think you know almost everybody here."

"You bet," Leo said as he went around shaking hands or giving hugs as needed. He was thinking to himself how much had changed in the months since the shootout, starting with Jake's new undersheriff, Steve Garvey. Then to Mason Peevy and Butch Harlowe—both mostly recovered but desk jobs only for a while yet.

Next was Matti Scully, his replacement as the new sheriff of Rockbridge County. Johnny Dodd was her new undersheriff, and DJ Dunn was now Matti's chief deputy. He opted coming to work for Matti and for a more laid-back lifestyle.

Leo had been forced to retire after having a heart attack during his leg surgery, that, plus the loss of his two deputies had made the decision easy. He'd backed Matti, and she won the election easily.

The next hand he shook was Connor Hess's, who had also retired. Mostly so he could spend as much time as he could with his wife-to-be, Matti. Last was Jake's partner and lawyer, Jon Wayne Key.

Coming back to Jake, Leo said, "So you're not sure of this sheriff thing yet?"

Jake shrugged, answering, "It's been a real challenge considering the mess the last sheriff left for me to clean up," which got a good laugh from everyone around.

Connor said, "Very funny, smart-ass, just remember, you might not have won if I hadn't endorsed you."

"Not won?" Jake laughed. "You dumb-ass, I ran unopposed!"

"Okay, okay" came a booming voice from the doorway. "Knock that shit off. What would the kids think if they heard you two carrying on like a couple old hens?" The voice was Caleb Johnson's as he came through the door carrying a couple of bottles of Kessler whiskey. He went on, "I just had a round with the groom and his groomsmen. Now let's see if we can get a couple shots in before the shindig starts."

"Damn good idea," Leo said, then turning to Johnny and asking, "Would you do the honors?"

"You bet," Johnny said as he poured everyone's drinks.

After they all had their glasses, Leo said, "I want to propose a toast." He lifted his glass up, saying, "Here's to all those not with us today. May they watch over all of us here today for Tana and Benny's wedding and all the tomorrows to come."

There was a quiet round of "here, here's" then nobody spoke for a moment.

Finally, Johnny said, "Jake, I hope you don't mind me asking, but what happened to that asshole, Dean Chadfee, after we gave him to you guys?"

"Well," Jake said, looking at his lawyer.

Key said, "Jake, it's your call, but I'm sure you can trust this bunch."

Jake nodded and asked Johnny to shut and lock the doors. Jake pulled a long cord out of his pocket, plugging one end into a big-screen TV and the other end into his phone. "Thanks to this new tech stuff, I can check on that bastard any time I want. So here we go. This is coming from my island in the Bahamas. I lease half the island to the US military. It's divided by a patrolled electric fence." Jake continued, "The other half, Dean is on. It's surrounded by sheer cliffs all the way around with twenty-four-hour naval patrols at sea.

No way on or off. This is Dean's house." A picture of a small white house appeared on the screen. "It's kept at a constant 50 degrees year round. Outside temps vary from 40 to 105 degrees throughout the year."

"Why at 50 degrees?" Johnny asked.

Matti spoke up, "Survival temperature, right?"

"Very good, Matti," Jake replied. "You remember your Army training survivor temperature. Not comfortable most of the time. We limit Dean's clothing, and here's his bedroom. It's a wooden platform, hard foam mattress, a single blanket, and a small pillow." There was no other furniture, only a huge clock alongside a large TV screen. "I'll explain about those in a minute," Jake said as he panned to the living room, which had a single wooden chair by a little wood table.

Again, they saw a huge clock and TV screen on the wall, and another wall was covered with shelves filled with books. Therewere two other doors. "One of these doors," Jake said, "leads outside, the other to a small bathroom consisting of a steel stool, sink and shower, no tub. The water is kept at sixty degrees and undrinkable. You'll notice there are no windows and no kitchen. All the furniture is bolted down, even the pillow and blanket are attached to the bed.

"Now, first, the TVs," Jake explained. "Once each day at random times, a program runs telling about all the ones who died that day, good and bad. It ends with a shot of his brother's head on my truck seat." As Jake continued on, you could hear a pin drop around the room, everyone mesmerized by what they were watching.

"When I made the deal with Dean, I promised him a library full of books, and I kept my word," Jake said. "He has a complete library printed in Chinese. The only English book is that Bible on the table, which he has yet to touch."

Jake went on, "Dean wanted female companionship—he asked for six. So I went around to the federal prisons, found six lifers who wanted an easier life sentence. They stay in their own place by the fence, treated very well as long as they follow the rules. If they break even one, they go back to hard time.

"Now to the clocks." Jake paused a moment before continuing, "Three times in a twenty-four-hour period, they chime. The clocks have no hour hands on them, only minute hands. When those clocks chime, he has to go for food and drink. He has thirty-nine minutes round trip, a minute for each death he caused. It was timed for a brisk walk, so if he runs, he'll have more time to eat or get back. He is served the best food and drinks in the world. He can carry back whatever he wants, but the food and drink are only out for eleven minutes, and if he doesn't get back in time, he gets locked out, and it's very, very unpleasant outside. At night, it's the worst, as he's found out. Doesn't sound too bad, right?" Jake asked.

No one answered; some nodded, others shrugged, all knowing that Jake had more to say. So Jake went on. "Now, this is the fun part. There are four paths to the food, all the same distance. One will be a clear path to the food and back. On each of the other three, one of his girls will be waiting for him. None are allowed to speak to Dean. Each day, they are given a random shirt with their given tasks for that day." Jake showed a picture of six women wearing bright orange shirts with a different word in black on them. Two had *Whipper*, two had *Caner*, and two *Lover*. Hopefully, you can figure out their tasks."

"Matti can explain them to Connor," Jake joked, which drew a nervous laugh from the group and a scowl from Connor. Jake went on. "They change shirts and paths each time so Dean never knows what awaits him, and don't forget, his time is limited, and he can't leave the paths because their sides are electrified. Oh, hey, it's feeding time." They all watched as Dean came out of the house, pausing only a second to choose a path then taking off at a run. He got only a short way down the path when a tall tough-looking blonde blocked his path, her shirt said "Caner," and she was holding a four-foot bamboo cane, holding it tight and like she knew how to use it. As Dean approached, he slowed to a walk and kept coming, his head down and arms at his sides, the perfect picture of defeat. But then as the blonde lifted the cane to strike, Dean ducked and took off at a dead run, the blow missing him. The blonde chased Dean, but with no chance of catching him, she quickly gave up.

"Well, I'll be damned," Jake said. "Dean won that time, but I bet blondie won't fall for that a second time." Jake killed the picture.

The room was quiet until Johnny said, "Jesus, I almost feel sorry for the bastard."

"Not me," Leo said. Then he added, "After what he did, he needs worse than that!"

"Sorry, Sheriff Leo, sir," Johnny said sheepishly. "I did say *almost!* I hope he lives a long life on his island."

"Jake," Matti said, "I'm sorry to even bring this up, but if the wrong people found out about this, couldn't you be charged with kidnapping and stuff? Dean does have rights, you know."

"No, he doesn't. That's the best part." Jake laughed. "Dean signed a waiver and gave up citizenship to any country, and the Army and CIA are paying me to monitor the whole thing."

"Great," said Connor. "Our tax dollars at work."

"Well, just so you can sleep at night," Jake said, "every penny I get from this goes to the Wounded Warriors Project."

"That's my boy," said Caleb. "But that's enough of this serious shit. Remember, we got a wedding thing going on today."

"Shit," Connor and Jake said together as everyone scrambled to fix tuxes and get flowers back on. Jake turned to Caleb, "Did you see Nicki when you came in?"

"Yeah, he went to see Cammie in the cemetery," Caleb answered. Jake ran out of the church and across the road to the graveyard, heading for a good-looking black-haired nine-year-old, standing arm in arm with his mother, Cammie.

As Jake neared them, the young boy ran to him yelling, "Dad, are they ready yet?"

Jake gave him a hug, saying, "Almost, Nicki, almost. Now you run in and get ready. Your mom and I will be in right behind you." Nicki took off to the church at a run. Jake hugged Cammie and asked her, "Is everything okay?"

Cammie gave Jake a kiss, telling him, "I'm so happy, Jake, all because of you. Our boy loves you so much and you having my other Nikki brought here to your family plot so we can visit her grave."

Jake kissed her and said, "My pleasure, now why don't you head in and check on Nicki and Tana. I'll be in shortly."

Cammie just nodded, knowing why Jake was staying. She turned and walked toward the church. Jake turned back to the gravestone, saying to Nikki, "I hope you like it here." It had been easier for his lawyer, Jon Key, to get Nikki's body moved here and to have Cammie's name cleared than Jake thought it was going to be. Cammie hadn't asked Jake to do it, but was in heaven when he'd arranged it. Jake kidded her that he had no choice, that if they were going to go to Peru to hunt geese and quail, he couldn't have her thrown in jail!

Jake walked a few feet away, stopping at Korrine's grave and looking at the four smaller head stones lined up in a neat little row. "Hey, gang," Jake said, "I hope you didn't mind me bringing Cammie's Nikki up here to be with you guys, and I'm sorry I haven't been by to see you much lately or at the school, just been a lot going on lately. Cammie's a little spitfire like you were, Korrine, and then there's Nicki, and with me being sheriff and trying to rebuild the town and school, and Tana and Benny's wedding, well, I know you understand. Tell you what, you have mother nature send me a big buck next weekend on opening day of deer season. That way, I'll know you're listening. Anyways, I gotta go. Tana's waiting. Love you all." Jake reached down and touched each of the little headstones then stopped once more at Korrine's. "Honey, you would be so proud of our Tana girl. She's strong and pretty like you," he whispered, gently touching the headstone as he walked away.

Jake walked to the church, wiping the tears away that had slowly started down his cheek.

Tana was waiting just inside the church doors. She said to Jake, using the nickname she and her siblings had for their dad, "About time, Old Man."

"I'll old man you. Don't you know you can't talk to the sheriff like that? And what were you and Cammie yakking about when I came in?" Jake asked.

Tana said with a smile, "Oh nothing much, just girl talk. I told her how happy I was that you had her and Nicki and how Mom would have liked her too."

Jake fought back the tears as the wedding march started. "Thanks, honey, shall we do this?" Tana nodded and held Jake's arm tight, fighting back tears herself. Halfway up the aisle, Jake came to a stop. He'd looked up at the saints painted along the ceiling. Their faces had changed to Korrine's and the kids', and they were all smiling down on them. Tana asked softly, alarm in her voice, "Dad, are you all right? Is there something wrong?"

Jake answered as he started walking again, "No, honey." He looked up again at the ceiling; the original saints were there now. "No, honey, nothing's wrong. Not one damn thing!"

Later that night at the wedding dance, Connor and Jake watched the dancers from a quiet corner. Connor said with a grin, "A great wedding, huh?"

"Not bad," Jake answered. "Our kids make a great couple, and you should be happy. I paid for the whole thing."

"You're the rich parent, remember, but I and the kids do thank you," Connor replied.

"Listen, Jake, now that we're alone, I need some questions answered. First, how the hell did you get Dean to give up his citizenship?" Connor asked.

"Greed," Jake replied. "Simple greed. I put a million dollars in a Swiss bank account in his name. He can check it each day and see it grow."

"I'll be damned. Greed, it makes sense. Now, cousin," Connor continued, "nobody else in the world knows you like I do, not even Caleb. So tell me, how long you really going to keep Dean on that island of misery?"

Jake took a moment before answering, then said, "The day he doesn't check his money and opens the Bible instead, I'll fly down and arrange different accommodations."

"With a man like that," Connor said, "it might take a lot of years." Then Connor added, "As long as you're coming clean with me, what's all this God talk lately and even going to church once in a while? I thought Jake O'Nell didn't believe in God or church?"

"Well," Jake said, "I got to thinking, I've seen what hell's like and met the devil a time or two, so I figured if they're real, maybe

God and heaven are too. To balance things out, if you see what I mean?"

"Makes sense to me," Connor said. Then asked, "I saw you by the gravestones today, Jake. You still talking to ghosts? Not that that's a bad thing. Hell, I still talk to Hazel now and again."

Jake leaned forward. "You are one nosy bastard, but yes, I do— not as much as I used too. Sometimes it just feels right, okay? Any more questions I can answer for you, or can I go dance with my daughter?"

"Just one more thing," Connor added. "Jake, if you pull anything on me again with anything, I will so kick your ass! Got it!"

"Not that I'm scared of an old retired sheriff," Jake said with a grin. "I got it."

It was then that Johnny, his fiancée Nori, Mason, and Mae walked up to them and said, "Connor and Jake, we just want to thank you two for all you've done for us. Helping our dreams come true."

After all the hugs and handshakes, Connor said, "No problem, you kids deserve it."

Jake smiled and said, "That goes for me too. You've earned it."

Then Johnny, who was more than a little drunk, said, "No offense, guys, but for being older like you are, you sure have a couple of hot gals" as he watched Cammie and Matti on the dance floor.

Nori said, "Johnny, watch your tongue. Go get me a drink, right now!"

"Okay," Johnny said sheepishly, taking off with Mason and Mae. Nori turned back to Jake and Connor. "You'll have to forgive Johnny. It's the beer talking, but he's right, they are hot."

Connor looked at Jake and said, "Those kids are right—they are hot. We're lucky bastards, you know that?"

"I know," Jake said with a grin, "I know."

Opening Morning

"Shhhhh. Nicki, there's a deer coming," Cammie whispered and turned toward Jake. "Is that a buck to shoot?"

Jake had spotted the monster whitetail coming a few minutes earlier, knowing he was seeing the biggest buck he'd ever seen—and maybe would ever see the rest of his life. It was right then Jake knew he had his answer from Korrine and the kids.

Nicki whispered, "Dad, are we going to shoot him?"

Jake answered, "Not this time, Nicki. How about we take that big fat doe behind him. Fresh venison steaks on the grill tonight!"

Jake looked up to the sky. Just before firing, he thought to himself, *Thanks, gang, I love you too!* Tears slid down his cheek as his finger squeezed the trigger.

About the Author

Photo by
Cindy McCullick

The author lives in rural Wisconsin with his wife and family. He's had some wild times on this journey called life, from hunting rattle-snakes and fishing with dynamite to having more than one brush with death and laughing about it afterward—and now writing books that once you start to read, you won't want to stop, stirring your emotions along the way.

CPSIA information can be obtained
at www.ICGtesting.com
Printed in the USA
LVHW110533121218
600165LV00001B/261/P

9 781641 387064